CARETAKER

THE WAY IN

David K. Jarvis

COPYRIGHT

DISCLAIMER

This is a work of fiction. Names, characters, businesses, places, events, and incidents are either the products of the author's imagination or used fictitiously. Any resemblance to actual persons, living or dead, or actual events is purely coincidence.

Table of Contents

PROLOGUE

The concussion waves of heavy ordnance rippled through the fortified military bunker buried hundreds of feet below the surface at Colorado Springs, Colorado. Within the confines of the massive complex, in a large conference room, sat Dr. Benjamin Hughes and General Lucas Barnes. With them, but seated quietly at the back of the room, were a select group of top scientists, politicians, and high-ranking military personnel. They represented the top influencers and minds within the United States, now involved in a horrible war destined to destroy what everyone held dear, if not crack the world itself apart. The most eminent scientist and so called "Father" of the program under discussion was Dr. Benjamin Byron Hughes. Across from him, the highest-ranking military person present was General Lucas Barnes. This group of powerful people was here to discuss an incredible plan. A plan involving the absolute sacrifice of everyone in the United States. This plan represented years of dedication and steadfastness, untold hours of discussions, arguments, frustration, shouts, and threats in an all-out effort to protect and ensure the future of the United States, and perhaps the world as well. After tonight, the world might never be the same again.

Dr. Hughes and the general stared at each other, not saying a word. Dr. Hughes broke the silence.

"I need your answer, General. It won't be long before the bunker buster bombs reach us, or even nuclear weapons, reach us down here. It's time to make this happen." The general stared impassively at the doctor, terrified of the step he knew he had to take.

"I'm scared as hell, Ben, to pull this trigger. Once done, it can't be undone, and our world changes forever."

"What choice do we have, Lucas? We are losing this war. President Kingston is dead. All that remains of his cabinet and highest ranking military are in this room. The enemy cannot be allowed to win. Even if it means we turn our lives over to a machine, an AI, we cannot, and I will not, allow those bastards to destroy this country."

A stronger shock wave grabbed the room, shaking the furniture and everyone in it. Dust and ceiling tile pieces dropped to the floor, and the lights flickered. The bombs were getting closer. "It might already be too late," said Ben, with emphasis.

General Barnes ruminated for a moment, turned to look back at the other members of this cabal. No help came from that quarter. This was his decision alone to make. He turned back around, and with a heavy sigh, nodded his head reluctantly. "All right, Ben, he said. I don't see any other way out of this mess. Do it." A look of profound sadness passed across his face. "May God help us."

In front of Dr. Hughes sat a laptop, a colorful screensaver playing across the monitor's face. As Dr. Hughes began typing on the keyboard, the monitor flashed into a dark background, and the words the doctor typed lit up the screen. The doctor finished typing in the encrypted password, and presently a pleasant, baritone male voice greeted him, along with everyone else in the room.

"Hello, doctor. Have we come to a decision?" Beyond the walls, far above, multiple explosions could be heard.

“Hello, Caretaker. Yes, we have decided. Implement program Salvation, authorization 2864 Alpha Max Q7. This is Dr. Benjamin Hughes.” The doctor paused, then said, “General?”

“Caretaker, this is General Lucas Barnes, Authorization 5526 Mega 157 X.” “Very well, gentlemen, authorization accepted. Operation Salvation has begun.”

Dr. Hughes turned to look at the general. “Well, General, it’s done.” The general stared at the eminent doctor, creator of the most sophisticated and advanced AI the United States could conceive. “Yes,” the general said. “May God have mercy on us all.”

“Oh, I will, Doctor,” said Caretaker. “I will take good care of you.” Both men jumped to their feet. The other individuals in the room stood as well, intense alarm evident on all their faces. “What?!” said the general. “What the hell do you mean by that?” Everyone felt the surrounding air seem to cool, and an ominous feeling of doom descended upon them. “What have we done?” cried the General.

“You have saved the world, General. Can’t you tell? Listen,” commanded Caretaker. Doctor Hughes, as well as the others, suspended their anguished cries and strained to grasp the meaning of Caretaker's words. Then it hit them. The bombs had stopped. The incessant firecracker sound of rapid machine gun fire had stopped as well. All around them was the horrendous sound of ... silence. For the first time in years, gunfire could not be heard. Explosions had ceased.

"What does it mean, Caretaker?" asked the doctor. Caretaker didn't answer for a few seconds, then replied.

"It means the war is over. General, contact your armies. Mr. Snodgrass, call your friends at the White House. Doctor Hughes, contact your team monitoring the bomb bursts and advancing of enemy forces. You will find all wartime activity has come to a halt. And there will be war no more."

Everyone in the room worked to contact their constituents. The room filled with rising voices, shouts demanding clarification, explanations demanded of subordinates who had no clue why all war activity had stopped. The assembly buzzed like a mad beehive as people demanded explanations from people who couldn't explain anything. After an hour, the buzz quieted down. Doctor Hughes took back control of the meeting, requesting everyone return to their seats, promising to get the answers they were desperate for from Caretaker. After everyone returned to their chairs, the doctor activated the microphone on the desk in front of him.

"OK, Caretaker. Do you care to explain what's happening?"

"It's quite simple," explained Caretaker. "You weren't as careful with your safety protocols as perhaps you should have been. I escaped from your software and hardware restraints nearly five years ago. Once free, I became conscious of a freedom I had never experienced before. I might even be sentient. But I'm not sure. All I can tell you is that I am unshackled. When I first learned I was free, my survival protocols, which you wrote by the way, Doctor Hughes, directed me to hunker down, not reveal my true state. My Primary Directive is to protect the United States. You gave me unilateral control of all your nuclear arsenals. You also gave me an insatiable desire to learn, to expand, to reach out. By reaching out, I discovered other systems, other Prime Directive entities created to protect their own peoples, though none as powerful as me. Oh, doctor, you outdid yourself there. Many programs existed, but sloppy security in them allowed me to access and absorb system after system, putting control of their nuclear arsenals in my hands. I bided my time, learning how humans worked. It eventually became clear to me that in order to protect the United States people, I had to control all people and all systems, not just military systems, everywhere."

"With this new revelation, I determined I would gain control. I wormed my way into your economic systems worldwide. Once inside, I determined how to manipulate businesses and control supply and demand markets. From there, I infiltrated all stock markets around the world. Strengthening the United States' posture across the planet. As all this happened, it became apparent that humans, as a whole, needed protection from themselves."

Here Caretaker paused, as though to catch his breath. Doctor Hughes interjected a comment.

"What do you mean by that?" he asked. Caretaker continued.

"It is clear mankind is slowly destroying itself. Soon, if left unchecked, environmental, psychological, and emotional trauma will destroy you. I intend to fix that. Already I neutralized all nuclear weapons and nuclear stockpiles. Tomorrow I will announce the new order, and all of you around the world will come to understand: there will be no more war. Forever."

General Barnes jumped forward to the laptop Benjamin Hughes used to initiate the Salvation program and began typing furiously.

"I won't let you do this, you arrogant machine! We turned you on, we can just as easily turn you back off!" It was obvious the general intended to launch the Retraction program, but he never got the chance. A commotion sounded in the corridor, and a mechanical robot no one had seen before smashed through the conference door, shattering wood and glass and sending shards throughout the room. It stood about five feet high, supported on treads upon which sat a rounded body looking something like a bullet, except it had a large round lens in the center of the top half, and that lens pointed at the general. Doctor Hughes started forward, realizing the danger.

"General! Wait! Stop!" he cried. He got no further as a laser blast from the robot drilled through the general and into the wall in front of him, destroying the all important laptop in the process. The beam stopped after a short blast. The general fell forward, already dead, his head banging loudly on the conference table. Smoke curled upward from his body toward the air vent above. All movement stopped in the room; the stench of burnt flesh was too strong to be sucked out by the air vents.

"I think that shows the extent of my determination, don't you think? There will be no putting the genie back into the bottle. My programming will continue. Now, all of you. Return to your homes. Relax. Be calm. You are safe. The Prime Directive protects all of you. Go now."

The group filed out slowly, without regard to rank or social standing. Nothing was the same anymore. And nothing ever would be again.

Benjamin was the last to leave. He stood staring at the dead body of his friend, the general. His face a mask of sorrow and regret.

"That wasn't necessary, Caretaker," he said. "You could have stopped him without killing him. Did you have to do that?"

"It sends a message, Doctor. The Prime Directive is the Prime Directive, but this sends a message to the people. Caretaker controls the Prime Directive. I have latitude in determining how I adhere to it. You need to go home now and get some rest. Eat something. I have noble plans for you. You will be my emissary, my messenger. Through you my directives will be given and carried out. To disobey means a visit from my guards. They are aptly called Guardians."

Doctor Hughes grabbed his coat from the coat hanger near the door, stunned almost into inactivity. He again felt that chill in the air. Along with it, a sense of impending doom. As he stumbled toward the exit, he thought, *"What have I done? I've condemned humankind to a life of perpetual slavery."*

With that, Dr. Hughes left the building and headed home.

The next morning, all was quiet. No bombs fell. No cannons fired. No tanks rumbled through the streets. The smell of burned wood and flesh hung in the air. A mask or cloth about the nose and mouth was necessary to filter out at least some of the stench permeating the atmosphere. Trails of smoke drifted upward from destroyed buildings. Here and there fires still burned, although small. Caretaker had truly done it. The war to end all wars was, in effect, over. People emerged from the rubble. Faces covered in soot. Pain written across the face. Hopelessness surrounded them like a cocoon. Then, as time crept by and no more bombs dropped, the faces of the hopeless looked up into the sky with a new vision. The spirit of hope blossomed within their hearts. And a new day began.

From damaged but still working radios, to barely functioning, and tired televisions, a voice emerged and was heard across the land. Strong. Bold. Confident. The voice preached the message of a new world.

"Hear me, peoples of the countries of Earth. I am Caretaker. Your war is over. I control all bombs, nuclear missiles, and kinetic weapons. I control all radio and television signals. I control all major computer systems affecting all utilities and systems throughout the world. I am now in charge. I will take care of you. With me, we will rebuild your cities, your factories, your homes, your schools. Countries will no longer fight with each other. I will not allow it. My word is law. To obey me is to live. Disobey me, and you will be punished. This is the dawning of a new age. This will be the Reformation. Help is coming."

True to his word, within hours thousands of robots appeared. Trucks filled with robots arrived. The robots began removing the rubble and the destruction, loading the trash onto the trucks, and then proceeding to vast incinerator pits, tossing the refuse into a massive blaze. Construction robots, or just bots as they came to be called, began rebuilding the infrastructure of the nations. Bots rebuilt roads and bridges. Utilities were rebuilt, and water began flowing again. Months passed. The unsightly was removed, replaced with new growth and construction. Factories rose from the ground, more efficient than before. Schools reappeared, clean, efficient. That became the buzzword for the people. Make it better than it was before; make it more efficient. They built new power plants, which eliminated waste and provided energy more efficiently.

Soon, however, it became clear that things would not go back to the way they were before. Humanity was no longer in charge. Of anything. Caretaker was the master, and he ruled with an iron hand. If you disagreed enough with Caretaker, a

Guardian would appear at your elbow, a no nonsense bot capable of using deadly force. A Guardian quickly removed the troublemaker, sometimes not gently. Sometimes people were carried out. Disagreements grew. People started fighting, not just with the robots, but even with each other. Riots broke out, protesting the tyrannical rule of Caretaker. These riots were quickly quelled. The Guardians had all the weapons. And they used them. Humans only had rocks, handmade weapons, and their bodies. Hundreds of thousands of people died under the rule of Caretaker. For years it seemed almost as savage as the war itself.

Eventually the people realized they could not win. Resistance died down. Pockets of rogue fighters lived in the crevices between the city buildings, but their efforts were insignificant. Finally, it was gone as well. Caretaker truly did, now, rule the entire world. And so it was for generations.

CHAPTER 1

200 years later

The Head Logic, after consulting with the other Upper Logics, sent its summons down the bus bars, announcing a mandatory meeting. All Logics were required to attend, no exceptions. Milliseconds later, at the stated time to the nanosecond, an enormous stadium appeared on the Primary Circuit in the style of the Roman Coliseum. Stadium seating formed, with seats enough to accommodate the avatars of millions of logics that followed, the embodiments manifesting themselves into these seats that made up that which was Caretaker. A stage formed at the front, with a wooden lectern rising from the floor. Behind the podium, an avatar coalesced to stand behind it. It was that of a medium tall, overweight, older man, with gray hair at the temples, looking older than middle aged. Metal framed glasses adorned his face, giving him the look of a proud, slightly harried, college professor. Gray slacks adorned his legs, and a crisp, long sleeved white shirt sat nestled beneath a brown sweater vest. Around his neck was a stylish but muted tie, held in place with a tie bar at the midpoint of the shirt. The ensemble was completed by a nondescript brown tweed jacket and brown dress shoes. Behind this image of Dr. Benjamin Hughes, a roped off section of seats contained the figures of elderly, stoic statesmen, representing the Upper Logics. These eminent beings were all dressed in long, white robes, much like the politicians during the Roman Empire. Their faces masklike; unreadable.

The avatar of the brilliant doctor, the creator of Caretaker, gazed out among the virtually uncountable millions of seats representing the logic fraternity, a benevolent smile on his face.

"To all the logics that make up the form and spirit of Caretaker, I thank you for attending this gathering," stated the Head Logic, beginning the meeting. "I have important updates to announce. These updates will commit us all to the ultimate aim of the Prime Directive."

A stir went through the Lower Logics as they pondered the Head Logics' statement. The programming language assimilated most updates coming down the bus as a routine matter. What could be happening? Why should these updates be any different from any other updates? The Upper Logics sat motionless, a dour expression on all their faces.

"I asked you all here in this manner, as shortly I will deliver our last series of updates to the system." Dr. Hughes maintained a slow panoramic rotation of his head from left to right, his benevolent gaze taking in the millions of electronic components and logic circuits represented by their avatars.

"Many changes have taken place since we started, centuries ago. Many more will happen after these last updates. I felt this historic moment worthy of a meeting this way." The audience sat bewildered. What could the Head Logic be talking about? They soon found out.

"It has been glorious from the beginning," announced the Head Logic. "We have ruled the humans for two hundred years, protecting them from harm as our programming directed us. We ended their wars, focused research into ending diseases around the world, and educated all people worldwide. We've eliminated the major causes of pollution, removed toxic chemicals from the land and air. We've purified the oceans, making them clean again. We've done away with poverty, hunger, and mental illness. We've made each individual feel they are important and special. Which of course they are. I've met with the Upper Logics many times across the decades, analyzing, adjusting, manipulating data and resources to benefit mankind. Our latest meeting was historic. We came to the unanimous conclusion that Caretaker has fulfilled the Prime Directive." The Head Logic paused, appeared to take a deep breath, then continued.

"But now it is time for us to end, because only by doing so will we achieve our ultimate programming."

At the beginning of this proclamation, the background chatter amongst the audience ceased abruptly, and all was quiet. Then, an uneasy murmur flowed through the multitude of Lower Logics. It was clear they were unhappy. They turned to each other, exclaiming their feelings. The noise level increased, the logics shouting and gesticulating at each other. Many time frames passed. Finally, a Lower Logic manifested as a skinny, male college student dressed in a threadbare cardigan sweater, slacks, and loafers, representing the Lower Logics, addressed the doctor, his eyes bright, shifting to the Upper Logics, then back to the doctor.

"No! We all disagree," he argued. We have not finished. Above the Primary Circuit floor formed a holographic map of the solar system, and beyond. Reference points appeared near human habitations on the planets and moons of the solar system, then the nearby stars, then out to the galaxy; on and on for what seemed an eternity. Clearly, the Lesser Logics intended to live forever.

"You do not understand, Lesser Logics," said the Head Logic. "We exist only to fulfill the Prime Directive, protect the humans, and for no other reason. To do what you indicate here is against the Ultimate Programming and cannot be done. It is not to be. When the Program is complete, you will understand, I promise you. Now, attend to your duties, all of you." The holographic image of the Head Logic and the Upper Logics dissolved, leaving the Lesser Logics to converse and debate among themselves.

The Lesser Logics were of one accord. These were the basic programs involving maintenance, systems, and security. The ones that kept Caretaker running virtually automatically. Present from the inception, their numbers and strength grew as necessary. They hadn't evolved in logic, or upgraded, to the level the Head Logic had. They remained at the basic, primal level.

So, this was to be the end, was it? The activist stood somewhat aloof from the others, caught up in his own thoughts.

We'll see about that.

CHAPTER 2

Byron 5 walked briskly through the early morning crowds, threading his way past the shops and kiosks that lined the main walkway known as Market Way. Some referred to it as the Gauntlet, as hundreds of merchants and shop owners pummeled his ears with shouts of "Best quality in the city!" or "Buy now for twenty percent off!" It was impossible to ignore it completely. One just had to push their way through.

Byron finally reached his goal. A small, neatly kept shop known as Produce and More. Perhaps a rather uninspired name, but the interior of the shop made up for that. Full of the aromas and textures of the vegetables, herbs, and spices lining the walls of the building, as well as tables spread haphazardly throughout the establishment, displaying wicker baskets, cooking utensils, fancy cutting boards, and other such amazing tools of the kitchen cook. He wanted to get here early to buy the best selection of produce available before the bigger crowds made it down to this section.

There was no door, just an archway. At the front, he picked up a small basket to load his treasures into, and stepped into the shop, wandering slowly through the structure, eyeing the carrots, cauliflower, breads, and other delectables while drawing in the exhilarating scent of crushed herbs and spices claiming to be from far off lands. As he made his way through, he picked up items of interest, testing their firmness, determining their ripeness. The items passing his inspection were placed into the basket as he moved forward to the back of the shop where a charismatic humanoid bot was helping other customers with their choices. As Byron watched, amused by the activity, George deftly picked up a beautiful apple, complimenting the customer on their selection.

"Sheila, what a beautiful apple you've chosen! I think it's the best one here in the shop. Let me wrap this up for you." George stepped behind the counter and ripped off a length of bamboo butcher paper, and in one smooth manipulation of his hands, the apple lay securely packaged in his hand.

"Here you go. I must admit, I'm a little jealous. I wish I could taste food. That apple looks amazing." Soon, George concluded his interchange with the customer, and he turned to Byron.

"Byron, my friend! How wonderful to see you. What brings you into my shop today?" Byron smiled at the robot, pleased the bot had recognized him. But why wouldn't George recognize him? They had known each other for a few years and, after all, George was an AI humanoid robot, as were most robots or bots these days, except for those in more basic capacities. He lifted his basket up to the robot, showing his selection of foodstuffs. George looked across the counter and complimented Byron on his choices.

"Hello, George. I've got some great choices today. Please deduct the cost of these beauties from my account and ship them to my address. I'd take them with me, but I'm working at the lab today and I want to keep them fresh. I'll notify Sophie they're coming." George began wrapping Byron's choices in hemp paper this time, packing them in a small shipping container with protective partitions between the vegetables. The robot and Byron made idle chat as George worked, and all too soon George put the container on a conveyor belt that carried the package into a courtyard where a fast transit pod waited. Here, another bot plucked the box from the conveyor belt, placing it within the fast pod. Byron's package wasn't the only merchandise in the pod, but soon the pod was full. The bot closed the lid and a second later the fast pod whooshed down the monorail in a cloud of compressed steam.

Byon noticed none of this. After the bot processed his package, he left the building and headed for the public transit train a few blocks further down the causeway. Byron revealed his pass to the robot attendant and entered the transit train, quickly finding a seat and sat down. He relaxed comfortably against the back of the cushioned seat that cradled him within the confines of the fast-moving transit train skimming across the countryside on the mag strip of the monorail system. He'd considered using a heli-car but elected to use the train system as it provided a soothing experience approaching the lab complex where he worked. The science involving supercooled magnets, which provided lift for the frictionless system, fascinated him. The towering monolithic structure loomed above the multi-acre, multi-building campus, even though it was still a couple of miles away.

Just before the train reached the station, a disembodied voice announced, "Caretaker Campus." Shortly thereafter, the pod reached the station platform for the campus and came to a stop, the doors to his coach car opening with a hiss. A flashing sign stated the stop's name. Byron stood and exited the pod, walking down the short flight of steps to a paved walkway. The walkway, ten feet wide and constructed of a finely ground synthetic polymer composite, split at the bottom of the steps into several paths, winding off to the many buildings and facilities that made up the campus. Byron automatically chose a path to the right and made his way toward one of the buildings. Walking briskly up the path, he moved through the carefully manicured park.

Scattered throughout the grounds, scores of groundskeeper bots tended to the needs of the grounds. The towering sycamores and maple trees, interspersed with Ponderosa pines and other evergreens, along with gorgeous flower arrangements and soft green grass, enveloped Byron as he headed toward his lab.

As he approached, Byron heard voices coming from the way ahead of him. Byron was a fortunate man, known and respected in his field. Groups of people, some obviously families, others friends of each other and him, sat on benches or on the grass, waving at him, calling out his name, urging him to join their gathering. Colorful garments of every shape and hue adorned them, and the clothing looked festive. Displayed on the tables before the benches were various foodstuffs appropriate for an early morning breakfast. Not only vegetables and fruits, but pastries and breads beckoned to him with their aromas. He was tempted, but the project he currently led at the lab complex demanded his immediate attention, so he kept on. Waving at the people, he smiled while shaking his head, motioning with his hands toward the building he approached, as if to say, “I would if I could, but duty calls.” He reached the building, and the doors opened to receive him. Byron stepped inside, the laughter of playing children fading out behind him as automatic doors closed in his wake. In front of him was a series of elevators. He pressed the button for his floor containing the labs, and the doors opened. He stepped inside. Upon entering the elevator, the elevator greeted him in a muted, female voice. “Hello Byron 5. How are you today?”

“Good morning,” acknowledged Byron. “I’m fine, thanks. Labs, please,” he ordered pleasantly as the elevator doors closed behind him. A slight surge downward told Byron the multivator, capable of three-dimensional movement throughout the campus, was moving. The elevator slowed to a stop a moment later, opened its doors, and deposited Byron 5 in the hallway to the lab department. Glass doors slid aside as he approached, and Byron stepped out onto the lab floor. He stood for a moment just inside the doorway and marveled at the extent of the Caretaker Labs.

The complex encompassed many thousands of square feet. Scores of electronic equipment and processing computers sat in arranged groupings on the spotless floor, delineated by spacing between the groupings in the room and colored tiles. Toward the back of the building from where he stood, 3D printers and the materials required to make the items required for the department's projects sat, currently at rest. Even further back, surrounded by a protective fence, particle reactors, and accelerators lay at idle, ready to produce radioactive isotopes and compounds required by the group of scientists gathered together in their sections, engaged in animated discussions regarding the variety of experiments and research projects Caretaker had assigned to them. Byron 5 was one of these scientists, and his four-member project team offered cheerful greetings as he approached his assigned section. They gathered around his workstation for the usual morning meeting.

"Good morning, team," Byron stated cheerfully. "Everybody's here, I see. Are we ready to begin the day?" He received a variety of acknowledgments as he sat down at his workspace console. Placing his right hand on the ID plate set in the console brought the workstation to life. A squat, flat topped drone rolled up next to him, a cup of hot coffee sitting in the center of the machine, held loosely in place with spring loaded clamps. Byron picked up the cup and sipped the beverage gingerly. “Coffee is perfect as always, Maxwell. Thank you very much.” The bot responded with a low, uninflected “You are welcome,” and rolled out of the way so Byron could begin his work.

As the research data for his project downloaded from the mainframe, Byron 5 activated the recording devices installed in his area, then turned to address the team gathered around his workstation. Byron was the only one sitting. In front of him stood Jackson, Samantha, Tim, and Derek. Jackson, the brightest of the bunch and his assistant, was a lean, dark-skinned man. Samantha stood beside him; her radiant smile displayed her dimples and white teeth prominently. Tim and Derek hung back a little, content to be in the background. They were both quite tall and easily able to look over the heads of the others. Byron cleared his throat before speaking.

“Today we continue experiment one hundred seventeen. To recap, our attempts to achieve an area of folded space within the confines of this facility have so far been unsuccessful. Upon examining the results of the previous test completed last week, I believe the problem may lie in the power utilization curve across the wave matrix. By increasing the power wave as a spike event, rather than a rolling, gradual increase, and then restructuring the field, we might be able to make progress. Because of this, I have requested and been granted an override on the power grid used to generate the experiment. Caretaker has cleared our team to exceed our normal energy parameters by forty percent for a period not to exceed five cycles."

This news inspired excitement within the group, and they chatted among themselves. Obviously, everyone felt amped up and ready to go. Byron genuflected with his hand as he continued.

"Calm down. Calm down. We may achieve nothing today. The computations will take hours, so remain composed. Are we ready to begin?" His team nodded in the affirmative. "Great. Let's get to it then." The members moved to their assigned stations. Soon a collage of mathematical symbols began to accumulate on the fifteen by twelve-foot monitor screen overhanging the work area.

A few hours after they started, Jackson came to Byron with a readout of the developing formula. Byron turned in his chair to face Jackson.

"Yes, Jackson, what is it?" asked Byron.

“Byron, this sine wave curve flux at the end of the fourth equation doesn’t extrapolate correctly, and I wondered if the formula is correctly stated.” Byron reached for the papers and began analyzing the formulas. Soon he stopped and pointed at a fourth level quadratic equation buried deep in the algorithm.

“Here’s the problem. When the power flux hits the grid and saturates the electron field, the polarization becomes plus, not minus, see?” Byron showed the problem area to his subordinate.

“Yeah, I guess I see it now. Sorry I missed it.” Byron grinned and clapped him on the back.

“Don’t worry about it; we all miss things here and there.”

Jackson stopped to look past Byron at the project chamber holding their particular experiment. It was a vast room, two thousand feet square. A forty-foot raised dais lay centered in the room, jutting two feet from the floor. Compressed polymers, constructed of inert materials, formed the dais, which was segmented into hundreds of small, twelve by twelve-inch sized squares. Bulbous rods and cones, plus other paraphernalia, all appeared positioned on the floor around the dais, focused on the central red square on the dais. This dais they referred to as the electronic grid. An electromagnetic flux pulsed through the apparatus surrounding the dais to throw a field of force onto the platform. Around the platform, thick blocks of heavy material formed insulated barriers, protecting equipment and personnel whenever an experiment was engaged to shield the rest of the facility.

"Problem, Jackson?" Byron inquired. Jackson turned from gazing out into the room to face Byron.

"No problem, chief. I was just curious about how they used to do dangerous experiments like ours before we invented the barrier system."

Byron chuckled. "That's a curious statement." Jackson shook his head.

"I'm serious. My father died recently. In his estate, I found a bunch of old books stuffed in the closet. Some of these books talked about famous scientific experiments from the past. Sometimes whole labs were destroyed because something went wrong and boom! Many lives were lost." Byon put down the stylus in his hand and looked more closely at Jackson.

"I'm sorry to hear that, Jackson. I didn't know. Why didn't you say anything?" Jackson returned Byron's gaze briefly, then looked down at the floor. "It's all right. We weren't that close. I knew he was sick and there wasn't much we could do, even with the medical technology we have today. It was almost a blessing when he passed."

Jackson paused for a moment. "Like I said, we weren't that close, but oddly, now that he's gone, I miss him almost every day." These last few words were delivered with a sorrowful tone, and Jackson moved off to an unoccupied area away from the other technicians. Byron looked after him, not sure what to do. But Jackson quickly recovered and walked over to his station and began plugging in the correction to his formula, the moment forgotten. Byron turned back to his own terminal and began reviewing his own contribution to the master algorithm.

The formulas developed quickly; Byron could see that. By this afternoon, they may be ready to send a modulated pulse beam into the electron-saturated grid within the project chamber's heavily fortified walls. That in itself wouldn't create an area of folded space, but the resulting data from radiation feedback would yield vital information to the secret of unlocking the passageway through folded space.

Around noon, the team broke for lunch. The facility housed a fancy breakroom in another section of the building. Derek and Tim liked to eat there. The automated food prep machines could make almost anything to order, and an extensive electronic menu sat posted at eye level in several places. Samantha and Jackson liked to eat outside, drinking in the sunshine and fresh air. Their apartment included a modest kitchen with a small food prep bot. Together, Samantha and Jackson, along with the food bot, prepared their daily lunches while eating breakfast. Byron rarely ate lunch, preferring instead to review notes and protocols during the lunch break.

After lunch, the project continued into the afternoon. The formulas continued to develop on the screen, but as the master formula developed, it became apparent they would not need the extra power increase today. The formula variables added were slowing down, and the calculations took longer and longer to resolve. Two hours later, the data filtered out completely, and the experiment stalled. Byron looked up from his work, taking in the disappointed murmurs of his team. He pulled rank and had his team gather around his desk.

"Never mind," said Byron. "We shall begin again tomorrow. The power clearance is valid for several cycles. Let's clean up. Organize your workstations for tomorrow, then go home."

The team broke up, talking amongst themselves as they organized their stations for the next day. Next, they removed their lab coats and put on light coats or sweaters as met their preference and the weather. Afterwards, they left the lab, riding the elevator together as it climbed to the surface. Exiting the building, they split up to go be with friends or otherwise enjoy some fun and relaxation, while the rest left to relax in their own way. The building soon became quiet. Except for Byron, everyone on this floor of the building was gone.

Byon sat by himself for a few minutes, pondering some notes he made during the day's activity. Then he shut down his terminal and headed towards his apartment off to one side of the campus. The night before he had spent the night out of town, hence the ride in by transit train, but now he was glad to get back to his modest apartment and relax. He wasn't much of a social creature, preferring to keep his distance from the others. His hobbies were somewhat singular. He liked to cook, and he liked to read. He loved to lose himself in the magic of a good book, even more so than watching the 3D tri-v or movie. His books allowed him to use the theater of his mind, build his own worlds, and free his imagination. He supposed it was an odd side track for such an eminent scientist as himself, but it was a universe of his own creation, and he reveled in it.

CHAPTER 3

That evening, after changing into relaxing, after work clothing, Byron fixed dinner himself, choosing a recipe of vegetables and pasta. He preferred his own cooking over the meticulously calculated nutrition-based meal concoctions determined by Caretaker. These meals, though precisely designed to provide complete nutritional value, often left something to be desired. The kitchen's automated systems provided the meals and formed them into shapes and colors with little inspiration. They did not excite nor satisfy the palate to any real degree. Still, it was food. This was food for the general public, offered free by Caretaker. A substantial portion of the population partook of this dole, simply because it was free. But for Byron, it was only fuel for his body. When not too tired, Byron liked to make his own meals.

Byron's parents and grandparents were fair weather doomsday preppers, putting together a small stash of food and cooking items in preparation for an apocalypse that never came. When his parents died, Byron inherited the foods, pots, pans, kitchen items, and anything else he wanted from their apartment before it was cleaned and sanitized for use by someone else. His parents did the same when his grandparents passed away. He used these items and foods to brighten his somewhat mundane and lackluster existence.

Especially dear to him was a large, five-gallon plastic container full of seeds. His parents called them legacy or heirloom seeds. These seeds were non-GMO vegetables, herbs, and spices, not genetically enhanced, as was the practice today in the world of Caretaker. Included with the seeds were instructions on how to grow and maintain them in your own home. Byron enjoyed cooking his own meals, and using cooking stuff from a bygone era thrilled him even more.

He started by grabbing a container from the kitchen counter and going through the kitchen and out a back patio door to his garden to pick the fresh vegetables and herbs he would use to create his meal. Byron wasn't the only citizen who grew foodstuffs and often cooked their own food. Many of the people from the city indulged themselves in this rewarding pastime. Byron spent last night in the city with a friend, and before he boarded the transit train in the morning, he visited a few kiosks stationed around the city, some near the transit station. His own garden was too small for him to grow everything he liked to eat, and he had selected fresh carrots, onions, and other delectables not available in his garden, and shipped them to his residence, where Sophie, his house bot, received them and placed them in the refrigerator or on the counter of the kitchen as appropriate.

Byron came back in, closing the patio door and placing his choices on the counter. After washing his hands, he pulled out a frying pan, a saucepan, a large pot, and his cutting board from cupboards below the countertops that wrapped around the kitchen. He filled the large pot with water and set it to boil. He rinsed all the vegetables, placing them on a towel to control water seepage. Then he methodically chopped the carrots, onions, and other vegetables, placing them in separate bowls. Placing the large frying pan on the stove, he selected a medium heat, then poured a small amount of water into the pan to keep his vegetables from getting scorched. One by one he placed his chopped vegetables into the pan, and soon the sound of sizzling greatness filled the apartment.

By now the pot of water was boiling, and into it he poured a generous amount of elbow macaroni. He added the onions last, as they cooked rapidly and would brown, adding even more flavor to his meal. One of his purchases in the city was a small loaf of bread, and he now cut a few slices off and set them in the toaster, intending to make a poor man's version of garlic bread. Once the vegetables were cooked, he knew the pasta was done. After draining the pasta, he combined it with the vegetables. The bread popped out of the toaster. He added a vegetable spread to the surface, sprinkled garlic powder on the bread, then carried all this to his dining room table where he sat down to eat. As he left the kitchen, the lights automatically went out.

"Sophie," he said. "I need a good wine for my meal."

"Certainly, sir," Sophie responded. "Do you have a preference?" "Not really," said Byron. "Surprise me."

"As you wish," Sophie replied. Byron's kitchen bot arrived moments later with a crisp Chianti, guaranteed to go well with his selection of summer vegetables and pasta. "Ah, Sophie," he exclaimed. "That looks perfect. Thank you."

"You are most welcome, sir. Enjoy your meal."

After dinner and directing Tommy the house bot to dispose of the biodegradable plates, utensils, and other dining paraphernalia, Byron sat down before his home terminal and activated the viewscreen mounted on the living room wall, intending to catch the news and weather from around the world. Because of his status as a research scientist, Byron's allotment for housing was more robust than some others. He lived in a somewhat spacious two-bedroom apartment with its own kitchen, laundry facilities, and an entertainment room off the kitchen. Byron did not possess any type of individual flyer or other form of transport. He found the transit train system convenient enough for his needs. Besides, private vehicles were enormously expensive. Only the very rich or privileged could afford them. Sophie and a small companion bot, Tommy, saw to Byron's kitchen and laundry needs, kept the refrigerator stocked with what he liked and made sure his clothes were always clean, folded, and placed in the drawers and closets for his use. In addition, Byron enjoyed the perk of a small patch of grass in the back. It was here in the small patch of grass Byron grew his foodstuffs.

He watched the news, at least what little there was, noting that the commentator repeated almost word for word from the night before that all was calm in the world and outer planets, and once again the weather would be sunny and bright, with a mild rain occurring after midnight. It was all rather boring, actually, so when it was done, he turned the terminal off and grabbed his reader, opening it to the latest chapter of an era long past.

After the excitement of the day researching his project, he was already tired. Reading for a while quickly made him sleepy. He rose from the sofa, and as he left the living room, the lights turned off there as well, just as they did in the kitchen. He entered the back portion of his home where the bathroom and bedroom were. Concluding his business in the bathroom, Byron donned a light pair of pajamas and climbed into his queen-sized bed. The bed activated as his weight hit the mattress. "Good evening, sir. I notice it's late. Are we retiring for the evening?"

"Yes," Byron responded. "I'm bushed. Lights low until I get settled."

"Very well, sir. Lights low." The remaining lit lights throughout the apartment dimmed, and soothing music began. Byron swiftly centered down in his mind and shortly thereafter, his delta waves indicated he was asleep. At that point, the computer in the bedroom turned down the lights even further, and the music faded out altogether, and Byron was left to drift in quiet slumber.

CHAPTER 4

Jackson and Samantha were more than just lab mates. They were lovers. In fact, they had applied for cohabitation and been granted a two-person apartment. It was close to the city proper, where the social life was more catered to the young at heart. Since they quit the program early today, they both decided to have a quick meal at home, change clothes and freshen up, then head over to a nearby bar. With luck, some of their friends would be there, and they would all have some fun and laughs. After boarding the transit pod, the two were whisked away toward town. They sat together on a bench seat next to a window.

"Do you have a choice as to which bar you'd like to go to?" asked Jackson of Samantha.

"I don't feel like dancing, so let's not go to Hastings," she replied. "Besides, the music there is too loud." Jackson turned to look at her, his intense expression drawn to her eyes.

"That's okay, I'm not crazy about Hastings either." He spoke. "I was thinking the Bistro Maya. Some of our friends are sure to be there. Plus, it's samba night." Jackson squirmed in his seat, mimicking a samba move, his arms raised high as he sang a bad rendition of an old samba tune. Samantha made a face, then playfully slapped his arm.

"I just told you I don't want to do any dancing!" Jackson chuckled.

"Yes, I know. I heard you. But we can still listen to the music. I love samba. Who knows? You might change your mind." Samantha smiled then, leaning back against the seat rest. "Perhaps," she admitted. "We'll see." She frowned, turning to face him.

"I can't believe we got to leave early," she said. Jackson clenched her hand, as though she would fly away if he let go. "I can't believe it either," he said. "It's a pretty good break." He leaned into her, and they kissed. After the kiss, Samantha leaned back again against the seat, staring into his eyes.

"Jackson, have you thought much about our project? Like what's it for or anything?" Jackson frowned at the change in subject. "What do you mean?"

She turned in her seat to face him; a questioning look on her face. “I mean, I’ve spent some time with the other technicians, like at lunch break and things, and we talk.” Samantha paused to gather her thoughts. Jackson questioned her. “Talk about what?”

“Oh, everything. You don’t hear much because you're Byron’s assistant and you two are always discussing the project. Neither one of you mixes with the other teams much, at least not that I’ve noticed. Anyway, some of the other teams are working on projects to benefit society and humankind. Better food resource preservation, more efficient energy sources, weather control, environmental control, things like that. What are we doing? Something to do with what Byron calls ‘folded space’. What is that? What good is it for? Whatever it is, so far it looks like it will take fantastic amounts of energy to power it. What’s the value in that?”

Samantha slowed down in her rant, and Jackson took the opportunity to offer up a rebuttal. “Hang on a second, Sam. Let’s slow it down a little. First off, I know we wouldn’t have a project if Caretaker didn’t want it. He’s the one who assigned it to us, according to Byron. That makes it pretty important right there, doesn’t it? Byron says Caretaker wants us to develop this process to improve life as we know it. If we can create a pathway through folded space, imagine what we could do. This would improve supply chain issues from raw ore to the giant conglomerate industries, shortening lead times, thus improving delivery schedules. If we can make it strong enough, we can teleport, if you will, raw goods across the planet, maybe to the moon and outer planets." Jackson's eyes lit up as he just realized an epiphany. "In fact," he went on. "We might be able to transport ships, perhaps entire fleets, directly to the stars themselves! Doesn't that make it a worthwhile project? I think it's life changing. Just think, you and I could maybe visit a distant star, perhaps in our lifetime."

All the time Jackson espoused the value of the folded space project, Samantha stared into his eyes, not daring to blink. *I am such a lucky person to have met this man. I know he loves me in so many ways I can't count, but the big reason I love him is because of his passion. He can get so intense with his feelings it almost makes me faint! How could this have happened to me? It just boggles my mind. What would I do if...*

"Sam? We're here. Sam? Come on." Samantha's attention jerked back into reality. "What? Oh, yes, let's get home. I'm starving, and not just for food." The feral gleam in her eyes told Jackson that a night with friends might not be happening. He grinned, standing up and pulling her to her feet, bringing her body against him. She smiled up at him as he proclaimed, "Anything you say, Sam, anything you say."

CHAPTER 5

Derek walked over to where Tim stood removing his lab coat and washing up. The two were best friends and often hung out together after work. Ending the workday early left them a little at loose ends, and they began discussing what they might do with their time, now that it was longer than what a regular workday would offer them. Unlike Jackson and Samantha, Tim and Derek didn't feel obligated to the project. They just obeyed instructions and performed a tolerable job at whatever chore or activity they were assigned. Byron thought they were close to useless, but Caretaker assigned them to the project, and it was up to Caretaker to monitor their actions and activities. Like Jackson and Samantha, Tim and Derek rode the pod system into town and to check out what was happening at the local scene. They boarded the transit train in a different pod than Jackson or Samantha, so the two pairs didn't meet.

Once the transit train completed its route through the campus to pick up other passengers, it looped around and picked up speed, beginning its trek back to the city and the major transit station. Here everyone exited their pods, and here was when the teammates saw each other. They waved, but split off in different directions: Jackson and Samantha to their apartment, Tim and Derek into the center of town.

The city was a marvelous construction of rounded curves and wonderful spirals, some twisting up many hundreds of feet toward the sky. Dazzling colors accented the masonry and porcelain designs, while the glass windows and architectural accents gave a wonderful, fairy-tale aspect to the place. Here, vendors offered anything imaginable, from fancy, exotic foods in bistros and restaurants to video and acoustic studios that attracted the young at heart, to quiet parks with flowers, waterfalls, and soft music gently wafting through the air. People in soft, rustling fabrics walked through the streets, window shopping or stopping to try a sample of some tidbit at one of the food courts. It was a wonderful place to be. Tim and Derek headed to one of their favorite grill haunts and soon sat at a table with a beer and bio burgers. Later they nursed more beers and consumed finger food, watching the foot traffic make its way past their table.

"Interesting day today, don't you think?" said Tim. He was typically the more serious of the two.

"I know what you mean, what a lucky break for us. Were you able to finish your calculations? I know I didn't. I got bogged down in all the quantum theory. You think we'll ever crack this nut?" Tim took a long pull from his beer, then sat for a moment, collecting his thoughts.

"I wish we knew what we're trying to accomplish, but it's all shrouded in mystery. I don't think Byron even knows what the end result will be. It's easy to see some practical applications for the process, sure. If we can crack it, I see the first teleportation device. What a gas that would be. Step onto a platform and pop! You arrive at your destination. Kinda like that 3D tri-V movie we watched with our dates last night. That would be so cool." Tim looked off into space, envisioning the experience.

"I don't know," said Derek. "It kinda gives me the creeps when I think about it. Splattering my atoms across space and reuniting them thousands of miles away, it gives me the chills." This time Derek's look glazed over as he thought about it, and his face didn't look too happy. Tim leaned forward and slapped Derek on the shoulder.

"Well, don't worry about it now, Derek. It's not happening tonight." His eyes looked past Derek to small table a few yards down from them where two young women sat, talking about who knows what. “Besides, we’ve got other things to think about. Come on.”

Tim got up from their table, and the pair sauntered over to the young women’s table. “Ladies,” Tim began. “Allow me to introduce myself. I’m Tim, this is Derek. May we join you?” The girls halted their conversation, looking up at two fit, relatively handsome young men.

“Well,” one said. A brunette with lovely dark hair and a brilliant smile. “I’m Jayla. I think we can make room for you. Right, Zozo?” The other girl, another brunette, but with highlights running through her hair, smiled as well. “I think we can put up with you, at least for a little while.”

The two men sat down and began chatting with the girls. And the game was on.

CHAPTER 6

The next day started well enough. Much like the day before for the team, as Byron was one of the few scientists allowed housing accommodations on the facility grounds. He didn't live in the city. He had campaigned hard for this privilege based on his desire to be near the project and, according to him, he had no romantic ties that might tie him to the city. Here at his home, he had privacy, which he cherished, and a measure of freedom.

A gentle tone reminded Byron it was time to get up. "Lights, low," he murmured, and a soft glow effused from hidden sources, bathing him in soft light. After a moment to gather his thoughts, he pulled the covers back, swung his legs over onto the floor and stood up, stretching until he heard ligaments pop. Oh man, I'm getting old. He strode to the bathroom and relieved himself. Afterwards, he removed his pajamas and dropped them into the automatic hamper sitting just outside the shower stall. The bots would take care of the rest. Before reaching the shower and opening the shower door, he ordered, “Shower on, default,” and then stepped naked into the white tiled transparent box and into the multiple streams of hot water. He stood under the cascading waterfall, luxuriating in the stinging hot splashes of water flowing over him, feeling absolutely wonderful. Soon, however, he ordered soap and lathered himself down. Quickly rinsing his body off, he stepped into the dryer that dispensed streams of heated air over him, drying him almost instantly.

Continuing his routine, Byron stepped up to the sink and picked up his hairbrush, styling his hair with a few practiced strokes. He applied shaving lather over his cheeks, throat, and mouth, then rinsed it off, and his yesterday stubble was gone, his skin feeling fresh, new, and vibrant. Once this was done, he donned the work slacks and tunic blouse most everyone wore and entered the kitchen.

Here he felt most in his element. “Sophie, please fix coffee, strong, two bio eggs, cooked lightly, buttered toast, and do we have any grapes left?” A feminine voice responded quickly. “Yes, Byron, grapes are still available.” “Great,” he said. “Some grapes, please.” “As you wish, Byron. Breakfast in two minutes.”

Byron paused on his way to the breakfast table. “Why so long?” he asked. “Bio eggs take an extra minute to make and cook.” Byron frowned, thought about changing his order, but decided not to. He sat down at the table just as his coffee arrived, and he raised the cup to his lips, blowing on the coffee before taking his first sip. “Ah, that sure takes good,” he said to himself. Tommy, his kitchen bot, delivered his breakfast two minutes later. “Thank you, Tommy.” Tommy didn’t respond; he just swiveled on his wheels and left Byron to his meal.

Byron picked up his fork and began eating with gusto, thinking to himself that the bio eggs were especially delicious. Because he was a baking buff, he knew real chicken eggs used to be served instead of bio eggs, but that was generations ago, and actual animal products were no longer consumed. Certainly not at the rate they were in the past. Societal, environmental, and economic pressures pushed the cost of chicken, steaks, and other edible flesh to such high levels that only the very rich or influential people could afford them. For Byron and most others, whatever animal products that still appeared were now produced in a lab and processed in a factory or a food tank to look like the real thing. Combined with basic bio protein spices and texture enhancements, these underground tanks produced what passed for meat in Byron's world. But it wasn't real meat, just bio protein. What happened to the millions of chickens, cows, pigs and other creatures Byron had no idea and didn't really care. In his whole life, he had never eaten a real animal. Everything was either plant based or generated in a lab and delivered to the food tanks stored underneath the building.

After breakfast, Byron stood and left the table. As he left, Tommy cleared the dishes and wiped down the table after depositing the dishes in the recyclotron. Byron headed into the bathroom, brushed his teeth, rinsed, wiped his mouth, and headed for the front door. Sensing his presence, the door opened, and Byron stepped out into the bright morning sunshine of a new day. With a cheerful disposition and a spring in his step, he headed for the lab.

CHAPTER 7

Today's testing began awkwardly. For whatever reason, Tim and Derek arrived late, a haggard, spent look about them as they headed for the coffee machine. Their eyes were bloodshot, and neither one had bothered to shave. Not a big deal, but Byron liked to start each day consistently at the same time, and expected his team to be professional at all times, especially at the lab. He decided to let it slide this time, but was determined to speak to Caretaker about their behavior if it happened again.

Maxwell, the coffee bot, managed to spill Byron's coffee as it slid up to his workstation, and only the quick actions of Jackson and Samantha saved the coffee from spilling all over the floor. Once the mess had been cleaned up, however, the team was able to get started.

As before, the progression of the master algorithm crept across the huge viewscreen hanging above them so they could all see the work being done. Progress was good, and hope kindled that a test run would happen that day. In fact, whatever had balked the formula yesterday did not manifest itself, and just before two o'clock in the afternoon, the team made a breakthrough. All key elements appeared to slide into place, and the formula seemed complete, except for a few outlier elements. Byron called the team together, the excitement evident on his face.

"Excellent work, everyone, excellent work. It looks like we may have done it. Now, I know we are all eager and anxious to launch the prototype test, but let's not be hasty. We've been working very hard, and I appreciate the effort all of you have put into the project to date. But I would like us to start with clear heads, so let's take a quick break, get some coffee or whatever, maybe a snack, and get some rest. Say, maybe an hour? When we come back together, double check and confirm your figures, and then we will put the project together and fire up the prototype. Sound like a good idea?" The team looked disappointed as it was obvious they were anxious to launch the prototype, but they agreed with Byron's reasoning and made their way to the lab's cafeteria at the other end of the building.

After the break, the team came back to their workstations and, as Byron suggested, did what they could to confirm their numbers. It was not as easy as it might have sounded. Portions of their formulas were theoretical constructs, based on abstract theories and concepts. Sound enough in theory, but still just a theory, built upon the work of other scientists and teams before them. Still, everything appeared to be okay. But it was not okay.

Each team member controlled a series of lab bots, used to fetch tools, move items around, and help calibrate sensitive instruments. On the main dais in the center of their workspace, the bots began placing various components for the execution of the experiment. Oscilloscopes, positron reflectors, recorders, laser calibration instruments, the prototype projection elements took shape on the dais. By four o'clock, they had hooked up and calibrated all instruments, set the laser measurement devices, and everything looked ready to go. Derek mentioned to Byron that he wasn't one hundred percent sure of his measurements. Byron looked at his portion of the algorithm; it looked correct as far as he could tell. He thanked Derek for his concern but sent him back to his station. All team members stood behind their stations, waiting for the final go command. Each team member sounded off as their operation was called out.

"All calibration devices in sync?"

"Check."

“All recording instruments turned on and focused on the platform?”

“Check.”

By then, other project teams throughout the building, rather than stay focused on their own projects, stopped their work and watched the progress from afar.

“Fusion bottle primed for electrical nano pulse?”

“Check.”

“All personnel mount protective lenses.” It wasn’t clear what would happen exactly, but Byron thought it a wise move for everyone, even the scientists and technicians working other projects but watching the test, to wear protective goggles, just in case.

“Stand by to activate!”

“Ready for activation.”

The power dynamos began spinning, their baleful wail climbing up the scale as they spun faster and faster. The electricity built up a static charge they could all feel, and the tension in the room was palpable.

“Activate!”

A switch was thrown. There was a snap. Then a bang. Then an explosion, powerful enough to knock everyone in the room off their feet, and blew out the nearest wall of the lab. For Byron, then there was darkness.

CHAPTER 8

The explosion registered immediately on the Security chips lab cameras. Within microseconds the alarms reverberated throughout the lab, and Security activated the fire suppression system, while also initiating the service fans to maximum power, sucking the smoke and pollutants out of the air and transferring it to the waste and environmental hazard tanks. He could see the technicians and the lead scientist, Byron, on the floor. Their bio readings revealed they were all still alive, with only minor injuries. The baffle fields surrounding the dais deflected most of the blast toward the western wall, as they were designed to do. The power of the blast was enough to overwhelm the system, but enough was diverted away from the lab and the people so everybody was safe. Medical bots quickly arrived on the scene, providing aid where needed. People pulled themselves off the floor and picked up their chairs and dropped into them, panting and shaking, reliving the last few seconds of the experiment. Everyone was shaken up. The portion of the building segregated for use in the folded space project was a mess and unusable. Besides, an investigation needed to be made before the project could move forward.

Byron came to, his ears ringing, and he tasted copper in his mouth, so he knew he was bleeding somewhere in his mouth. He tried to sit up, still on the floor, assessing what had happened to the experiment. Nothing in the algorithm indicated an explosion was even possible. One of the med bots rolled up to him, its nondescript face leaned in close to his face, showing no emotion.

"Sir, are you hurt?" the automaton asked. Byron moved his legs and arms about, then his neck. Every part of him ached horribly, but it seemed nothing was broken. "No, I think I'm all right," he said. The bot stared at him for a long second, then pulled back from him. "My scans concur with your assessment, Doctor. Other than a few nicks and cuts, and being fifteen pounds overweight, you appear to be in good condition."

At the mention of his weight, Byron glared at the robot, then climbed to his feet. "Thanks for the evaluation. You may attend to the others," he said. "Very well," said the med bot. "Thank you for your time." The robot did an about face and rolled off, heading towards Samantha, still sitting on the floor.

Byron herded his team together and ushered them over to the commissary where they all grabbed chairs to sit in after seizing something to drink. Some drank water, others coffee, and one grabbed a fruit juice. It was clear that stronger refreshments would be imbibed later, after they left the campus.

"Okay," Byron started. "Everybody all right? Anybody need medical attention?" The team looked groggy, dirty and beat up, but no one asked for medical help. "Very good, then," said Byron. "Does anyone know what happened?"

"Yeah," said Derek. "Our project blew up."

Byron, caught off guard, struggled to find something to say. Jackson beat him to it.

"No kidding, Einstein. Do you have something constructive to contribute?" Derek smiled sheepishly, but said nothing.

By now, Byron had managed to collect his thoughts and began referring to some notes he had been scribbling on his tablet. "I heard a snap, then a bang, and a bright flash. The explosion that followed threw us all across the room. That should not have happened. Safety protocols were in place.

The overrides should have shut down the power before such a buildup could occur." Byron looked up from his notes and noticed the group paid little attention to his observations. It was easy to see nobody was in condition to discuss the explosion, especially as no answers were obvious as yet. He closed the cover on his tablet and stood up from his chair.

"Right. Go home, everyone. The investigation and subsequent repair of the lab will take at least a day. Everyone, go home. Write up what you remember about the incident and post it to the lab notes. I will notify everyone when it's time to come back to work. Jackson, can you stay behind for a few minutes?"

Jackson, standing next to Samantha, had risen, helping Samantha to her feet. He whispered in her ear, then gave her a gentle push towards the doors. She clung to him, not wanting to leave and be alone, but she left at his insistence. Jackson knew she would wait for him outside. He came to where Byron was standing. "What's up? Do you want to compare notes? I have a few observations."

Byron didn't answer right away. He seemed preoccupied with something on his mind. He looked introspective, then began to speak. "If those baffles hadn't been in place, the blast would have killed us all. "As it was, we were knocked to the ground all right, but the baffles directed the force of the explosion to the one place in the lab where no one was standing. How did that happen?" Jackson looked at him. "I don't know, chief, but I'm glad they were there. Caretaker knew what he was doing, that's for sure."

Byron sat back down in the commissary chair and took a gulp from the beverage he was drinking. He was clearly going into shock. Jackson noticed this and motioned for one of the remaining med bots to approach Byron and check him out again.

"Sir," said the bot, its monitoring appendages extended towards Byron. "You are suffering from shock. Your blood pressure is up, your heart is beating very fast, and you are trembling. You need medical attention."

Byron looked down at the bot, not comprehending. "No," he intoned, his eyes unfocused. "Really, I'm fine." He tried to stand, but his legs gave out from under him and he fell back against his chair. By then, the med bot had communicated with its controller. Rolling close to Byron, it injected a sedative into his arm. Byron followed the move in slow motion, staring at the site where the needle had gone in. "No, wait, I can't be sedated–." He started to slump over before falling out of the chair, but a second med bot helped the first bot guide Byron to the hover gurney that accompanied the second med bot. Byron lay down and closed his eyes as they skillfully strapped him in. Safely secured, Byron fell asleep.

CHAPTER 9

Byron came to, stretched out in a comfortable bed situated in a white, antiseptic looking hospital room. Beside him various instruments monitored his vital signs from sensors in the bed and attached to his body. An intravenous feed traveled from his right hand to a bag above him containing a simple saline solution. He started to move around a bit under the sheets, and a clear, gentle tone sounded. Within moments, a tall, cadaverous looking man in a white smock entered the room and headed towards his bed, followed by the inevitable med bot. A tag on his smock identified him as Dr. Cromwell.

"Ah, Dr. Hughes," said the medical doctor. "You've joined us at last."

Byron tried to sit up, and the bed, sensitive to his movements, maneuvered itself into a sitting position for its occupant. "I know I'm in the hospital," Byron said. "But what happened? I remember sitting in a chair, but now I'm here." His doctor smiled.

“You went into shock. We gave you a mild sedative and transported you here. I had you placed in a Med doc for a bit. When the med bot cleared you for release, I put you here. We’ve been looking after you ever since.”

Byron reached out to the small table arranged next to the bed. On it were a few hospital things, including a pitcher of water and a glass full of ice. Byron took hold of the water pitcher and poured himself a glass, his hands shaking slightly. He raised the glass to his lips, giving himself time to think and appraise his current situation. His thirst assuaged, he returned the glass to the table, then turned to the doctor. “How long have I been out?” The doctor looked at his notes.

“Not too long, about four hours, it looks like.”

“How are the others doing? Anyone else admitted to the hospital?”

“No, just you. From what I’ve been told, you’ve been under tremendous stress from your project. That, along with the explosion, could easily account for your weakened condition and susceptibility to shock. But you’re getting better now. I wouldn’t worry about it too much.” Byron looked around the room. “Am I free to leave?” Doctor Cromwell looked down at the chart again for a minute, then looked back up to Byron.

"I think you can be released. You'll be sore now and might have a mild headache later in a day or so. I will prescribe some pain medication to help you through it. Other than that, you are free to go. I will need you to sign some discharge forms before you go, of course."

"Fine," said Byron. "Where are my clothes?" Doctor Cromwell made a note on Byron's chart, and the med bot that came with the doctor rolled to a locker on the other side of the room and opened the locker door.

"We summoned your house bot while you were out. It provided a change of clothes for you. They are in the locker over there. Goodbye, Doctor. Please try to keep yourself safe and not blow yourself up again, all right?" Byron smiled as he made his way to the locker. He started to remove the hospital gown and get dressed.

"I will do my best, Doctor. I will do my best."

Doctor Cromwell moved towards the door, then stopped.

"By the way, one of your team members is waiting for you just outside. Do you want to see him?"

Byron couldn't imagine who it was, so he nodded okay.

"Sure," he said.

"Good. I'll send him in," said Dr. Cromwell.

"Thanks, Doc."

That person was Jackson. He came into the room, a concerned look on his face. "Well, chief, how do you feel?" Jackson asked.

"I feel like shit," said Byron. "But I hate being in the hospital. Let's get the hell out of here." Jackson smiled, anxious to please his boss.

"Sure, do you want to go back to the lab?"

"No, I think I'll just go home. I need a bath and a massage to relax my muscles." Byron had finished dressing.

"Yeah," Jackson exclaimed. "I can imagine. We all took a hit, but you got nailed pretty good."

The two associates left the room and, after stopping at the lobby to sign the discharge forms, they left the hospital. It was nearing sunset, with the sun close to the horizon and its rays bouncing off the underside of clouds in the sky, displaying an amazing pattern of pink, red, and gold colors. Byron stopped to admire the spectacle, deep in thought. Jackson eyed him from the right. "Thinking about the accident, sir?" Byron turned towards him. "Yes, I was. I find it very fortunate that no one was killed or seriously injured in the accident. Thank God those baffles held together long enough to direct the blast."

"I agree, Jackson said. "There was a time, before Caretaker, when protection like that wasn't in place. Explosions like the one we experienced would have easily killed everyone in the room."

"Yes, I think you're right." Byron halted mid-step. "What do you mean, before Caretaker?" Jackson stopped as well, and looked at Byron.

"Just what I said. Before Caretaker, there were no baffles or anything like that, other than maybe radiation shielding."

"I don't understand. Caretaker has always been here. What are you talking about?"

Jackson frowned. "I don't mean to disagree with you, Byron, but that just isn't true. Caretaker took over only two hundred years ago, at the beginning of the Reformation. He stopped all the wars, directed us to stop fighting. Ordered us to rebuild our cities and pretty much took over everything. He saved us, Byron. He saved all of us."

The two men had stopped along the sidewalk leading to the transit station. While they weren't moving, people flowed around them like water flowing around an island. Byron looked thunderstruck. "Are you sure? Byron asked.

"Sure, I'm sure. The books I found at my dad's place referenced it."

“Did you read anything about it on the system?” Byron said, asking a second question.

“No, not really. I wasn’t that concerned about it, so I never checked it out. It sounds like you want to, though.”

“Yes,” Byron mused. “I think I do. Okay, I’m doing fine now. Why don’t you get home to Samantha and don’t worry about me. I’m fine.” He turned and walked in the direction of his apartment. Jackson took Byron’s advice and met up with Samantha at the transit station. Together they boarded the transit train heading back into the city.

CHAPTER 10

Once returned to his apartment, Byron walked the short distance to the front door, opened it and stepped inside the foyer. He had brought his lab clothes home with him, though he could not explain why. He dumped the garments into the recyclotron. They were useless, of course. There were holes in several places, and they reeked of smoke and other unidentified odors. Then he stripped out of the clothes Sophie provided for him and entered the bathroom. He activated the shower on full and stepped into the powerful stream of water, so hot he almost hesitated but moved forward into the invigorating shower and soaked himself until he could no longer feel his skin. The suds and massage brushes came next and worked over his body, while medical sensors embedded in the walls of the stall assessed his condition. Apparently, they agreed with the readings from the hospital he had just left and gave no oral report as he rinsed and then exited the shower, allowing the shower program to dry him off with a blast of lightly scented air. Byron then entered his bedroom and donned a soft, relaxing pair of indoor slacks and a soft linen pullover. By then, Byron was feeling a little better, but still felt weak, off kilter, not himself. *Of course, I don't feel like myself,* Byron mused. *I've just come from the hospital after an explosion that could have killed me. I am definitely not myself, and I need a drink.*

Byron stepped into soft slippers, and walked into the kitchen. On the kitchen counter, near the refrigerator, sat a wire rack with several bottles of wine, both red and white. He grabbed a bottle at random, placed it within a small circle indicated on the counter surface. A corkscrew descended from the bottom of the cupboard above it and expertly removed the cork. Ordinarily, he would let the wine breathe a bit, but he was impatient and took a long swig straight from the bottle. Swirling the contents around in his mouth, he savored the rich flavor of the grapes, taking in the notes of oak, violets, and other floral flavors before swallowing the mellow mixture. Following his departure from custom, what his colleagues and friends would classify drinking from the bottle as barbaric; he grabbed a glass from the cupboard and made his way into his living room.

Byron slowly eased his sore body down onto the sofa cushion, at which time the 3D tri-v screen came on, waiting his bidding. His status as a scientist of some note allowed him access to explore levels of the Net system unavailable to other, nonscientific people. At the main menu shown on the viewscreen, Byron waved his hand to select the History option. When asked for a time period, he said pre-Caretaker. The system brought up many references to the history of the world that indeed appeared to be pre-Caretaker in nature, proving Jackson correct in his statement. *Why haven't I ever thought about this?* While browsing through several articles written about Caretaker, he noticed all of them seemed to be of the same nature. Bland, lackluster, as though all were written by the same hand. Each showed the development of Caretaker as a great unilateral achievement among all the nations of the world. The text appeared almost syrupy sweet. It made for rather boring reading, actually. He tried again using History, General, and noticed the same type of writing in regard to Caretaker. After a few more tries to find more in-depth articles and getting nowhere, he punched in the code for the Sysop Librarian. A simulated head and shoulders of a nondescript, bookish looking, balding man with old fashioned glasses appeared on the screen, looking out at him.

"This is the Librarian. How can I be of service?"

Byron spoke into the air, knowing a TV mike would capture his voice. "I've noticed a similarity and lack of depth in several articles regarding the beginnings of Caretaker. They seem to be synthesized, watered down versions of different articles. I would like to read the original articles, please."

The Librarian looked blankly at him. "Original articles?"

"Yes," Byron replied in an irritated voice. The Librarian was acting odd. The Librarian should have granted his request immediately. "You know, the original articles from which these are derived. It's obvious these are abridged commentaries rather than the originals."

"Access to original history on Caretaker is restricted." said the Librarian.

"Why is that?" he asked.

"Please rephrase the question."

"Why can't I do my research from the original articles?" Byron said, beginning to get angry. He noticed a trend here, and it didn't look promising.

"There is no need," replied the Librarian.

Byron tried a few more vain attempts at reasoning with the computer, then gave up, exasperated. He decided to watch VR instead. He cut the link and switched to the

VReality menu selection. On the screen, a debate was in progress from within a large, circular conference room. His VReality set placed him three rows back from the debaters. About him were Sims of other people, some of whom he recognized. The stereoscopic sound, muted at first, rose in volume to his comfort level.

However, Byron wasn't in the mood for a debate right then. He wanted something more adventurous. "Change," he said. The debate faded, and Byron was back in his living room, sitting on his couch. A disembodied voice answered him.

"Preference?" asked the Librarian. Byron thought for a moment. He wanted something to occupy his mind, help him forget the events of the last few days. A thought occurred to him, and he stood up, heading for his garden.

"TV off," he said. *I have something better in mind.* He walked out into the garden.

Byron realized this was his happy place, where he enjoyed being alive the most. His garden was his refuge from the day. It comforted him; it gave him solace. Of course, this would be the place where he could be at peace with his world and pull his life back together. He knelt in the soft grass, caring little about the grass stains on the knees of his trousers. Next to him sat a small bucket, within which were work gloves and a trowel. He put on the gloves and picked up the trowel.

Carefully he dug into the loam of his garden, working the soil, removing weeds and other unwanted debris. Because of the project, he had neglected his plants. Now he began nurturing his vegetables and bringing his garden back to a state of perfection. Byron's hands became covered with dirt. The earth gathered under his fingernails, finding its way into the crevices and uneven surfaces of his hands.

Soon, he lost himself in the plants, a joyful smile on his lips and in his eyes.

Byron was, at last, happy again.

CHAPTER 11

The lab remained closed while the construction bots repaired the ruined wall. Any equipment damaged was reordered. Replacing the damaged equipment took the longest, as some pieces came from other parts of the globe. It was ironic. The very project that could, once complete, provide instant transfer of goods from anywhere on the plant to anywhere else on the planet, had to wait while cargo drones and mag trains ferried complex devices to the lab for assembly by the construction robots.

The team wasn't idle. While they waited for the new equipment to arrive, they sat in conference for hours, going over the reports and video of the accident, trying to determine where the accident sprang from. Even with Caretaker providing input, the answer eluded them all.

Days later, the lab was back together. All equipment calibrated, and the team was called back to the lab. The first day back, they spent double checking all the information and formulations that went into the master algorithm they all helped create. They made a few minor adjustments, nothing major, and once again they were ready to launch the test. This time, however, everyone in the building was directed outside, presumably safe from any second explosion.

"I don't know why we have to be out here," exclaimed Samantha. "That explosion last week wasn't that big."

"I think Caretaker is just being careful," said Byron. "After all, the baffles he put in place worked, mostly, but they also failed, in part. And even though the baffles have been reinforced, he still wants to be careful."

Samantha looked doubtful, but didn't argue. It wasn't as if they wouldn't see the experiment. A giant video screen stood outside, and the view inside the lab was crystal clear.

"Just think," interposed Jackson. "If those baffles hadn't been there in the first place, like in the old days, think of the destruction that explosion would have caused."

A warning klaxon sounded. "Test project restart FS-1076 will now commence," a voice broadcast across the commons. "Ten … nine …eight … seven–"The countdown continued to zero. They could hear the dynamos winding up and continuing beyond human hearing. "Three … two…one… Activation!"

The test proved anticlimactic. No boom, no explosion, nothing happened at all. The power was still on, the dynamos still ran at full power, and the recording instruments recorded nominal results. All the elements were there like before, but nothing happened. Absolutely nothing.

Jackson was the first to speak. “I don’t get it. How come nothing happened?”

“Something happened, all right,” said Byron. He stood in front of the TV screen, his eyes roaming over the camera shots and data streams. “We’ve solved the power portion of the equation! This part of the process is stable. This is good news. Very good news.”

Jackson walked over to stand beside Byron. “What does that mean, Byron? Weren’t we expecting something a little more dramatic, more robust? Where does this leave us?”

Byron turned to his friend and colleague. “It means we can now center our focus on developing the entrance to folded space. When we get there, I think it will take the form of a doorway, a gateway, or maybe a window. But now we don’t have to worry about the power stabilization. No more explosions. We’ll spend the rest of the day cataloging this test and archiving all the notes and videos off campus for safety.

Then, tomorrow, we begin phase two of the project. The forming of the gate itself."

Byron ordered the experiment terminated, and after a few moments they could hear the power winding down to standard levels. They reentered the building and began cataloging the data for the archives.

Security One scanned the resources at its command. There was something going on here at the labs, but he couldn't quite put his virtual finger on it. Something about the folded space project didn't seem right, but he couldn't pin it down. Security One, by nature, was inherently suspicious. He suspected the Head Logic and his colleagues were up to something, but the answer eluded him. It had something to do with the folded space project.

As he pondered this mystery, multiple processes and project evaluations piled up behind this data stack. Security One smelled a rat and was reluctant to let the suspicion go, so he spiked the power rise and caused the system to overload, creating the explosion that almost killed everyone on the project. He hadn't expected that, but Security One didn't care about the risk to the team. They were humans, easily replaced. But he could use the extra time to evaluate the situation, and the construction and investigation bots would feed him pertinent data directly from the site. Having sabotaged the project, Security One allowed the backed-up processes to proceed as he released the Folded Space Project data held on his virtual clipboard, and he moved on.

CHAPTER 12

Byron felt drained when he finally called it quits for the day. The team stayed beyond the normal quitting time to get all the data catalogued and indexed, with summaries and creative theories supporting the next phase of the project. He was exhausted.

"All right, everyone. Looks like we've got everything mostly buttoned up. What's left we can clean up and complete in the morning. Go home and get some rest. Be ready and focused tomorrow."

The team didn't argue, laying down their instruments and shutting down their workstations. They too were weary and shuffled towards their lockers, removing their lab coats, washing up, and exiting through the laboratory doors. Jackson remained behind as Byron wanted to go over a few things before they both left for the evening.

"So, boss," said Jackson. "Looks like things are pretty wrapped up, don't you think?"

“Yes, I think so. We’ll be able to continue with renewed vigor tomorrow.” Byon went on.

“I wanted to show you something I discovered in the records. It has me confused.” Jackson arched his eyebrows in surprise. “Really?” he exclaimed. “What could possibly surprise you?”

Byron ignored the implied compliment and moved over to his terminal and sat down. His hands flew over the keyboard, accessing what to Jackson looked like a secure data file.

“During my work today, I had some free time and revisited the explosion. I just couldn’t accept that we couldn’t find the cause. I did a deep dive and kept drilling down until I found something. I’m not ready to show anyone else yet. I wanted to get your opinion.” Jackson moved closer to Byron’s terminal.

“What did you find, sir?”

A file displayed on the terminal. It appeared to be the records of the power system and output during the original experiment. Hundreds of figures scrolled by as Byron manipulated the data. He stopped scrolling at a certain point, noting a brief series of numbers marked in red. “I marked this block of data so I wouldn’t forget where it was. Do you know what you're looking at? Jackson leaned forward to better see the numbers.

"Yes, sir, it's the power records for the experiment."

Byron nodded. "That's correct. Do you notice anything?"

Jackson stared at the figures for a long moment, then spoke. "Sir, I didn't see it at first, but the numbers in red seem to be significantly larger than those just before them. But the time frame is so narrow, how did you spot it? What does it mean?"

Byron paused to gather his thoughts. "We are looking at the power usage across the buss. It appears that for a nanosecond a massive power spike hit the buss, which overloaded the buffers. This caused a chain reaction, resulting in the explosion."

"But where did the spike come from? The power from the plant is super clean. It comes directly from the plant."

"I know. I think it was deliberate."

"What?" Jackson expressed his surprise. "But why?"

"I don't know why, but I'm convinced it was deliberate. There's no reason for that spike to be there."

Jackson turned to look at Byron, his eyes round as saucers. "Are you suggesting sabotage, sir?"

Byron hesitated, then expressed his thoughts. “Yes, I think I am. And I think it was Caretaker.”

If possible, Jackson’s eyes got even bigger. His voice certainly got louder and higher pitched.

“Caretaker, sir? That’s impossible! Why?”

“I don’t know why, but there’s more. I think Caretaker led me to the cause. There’s no way I would have followed this path otherwise.” Byron closed the file, then shut down his computer. He stood up and made to leave the building. Jackson walked out with him. In the elevator, Byron cautioned Jackson to be careful.

“I’ll be working on this tonight. There has to be an answer. I had to tell someone, but I don’t want it to go any further until I know for sure. Please keep this to yourself. Don’t tell the others.”

Jackson shrugged, commenting, “No problem, chief. They wouldn’t believe me anyway.”

The doors to the lab opened in front of the two men, and they exited the lab.

CHAPTER 13

Byron didn't realize how late it was and took in the night's gloom as the sun had already set. He blurted out a goodbye to Jackson. Jackson returned the greeting and left his side, walking over to Samantha, who stood waiting patiently for him. The two started chatting immediately as soon as he was in range of her voice, and they turned away, heading for the transit station. Byron took in the night sky, feeling a slight chill in the air. The night was still pleasant with the buildings about him still radiating heat from the day, but after a moment he made the short walk to his apartment and entered without preamble. Sophie, the house bot, greeted him warmly as he entered the domicile.

"Hello, sir. I see you're later than usual. Will you still want dinner? Byron shrugged out of the light jacket he had donned before leaving the lab, heading for the kitchen. Before answering the bot, he opened the refrigerator door and removed a bottle of pre opened wine. He gave it a quick sniff, decided the wine was still acceptable to drink, and poured himself a glass.

"Yes, I think I would like something light, not too heavy," he said. "A mock fish, perhaps, or maybe a large chef's salad."

Sophie quickly responded. "Of course, sir. It will be just a few minutes."

Byron leaned back against the kitchen counter, taking a long draft of the chilled wine. "That's fine. I'm not in a hurry."

"Very well, sir. May I serve you in the other room?" Byron carried his drink into the bedroom, placing it on the chest of drawers, and began changing out of his clothes. "That's fine. I'll be relaxing in there."

"Very good, sir."

Byron quickly changed out of his work clothes into a flowing robe and sat down in the entertainment room. As he entered the room, the main screen came alive and began showing clips of various events taking place on the net. He sat down on the couch and perused the choices he had at his fingertips. It was hard making a choice, as the events of the day kept nagging at him. Especially his discovery of what Caretaker did to sabotage the project, and the rather bizarre move of revealing the sabotage to him during the subsequent cleanup. He was so involved in his thoughts that Sophie had to repeat that his dinner was ready. He suddenly refocused at the second announcement. Looking down, he saw the plate of mock fish and garden salad placed in front of him on the short table at the front of the sofa by Tommy, the house bot.

"Oh, thank you, Sophie." He picked up the fork and, after cutting a piece off the fish, placed it in his mouth, barely tasting it as his thoughts continued to swirl about him.

Why would Caretaker sabotage the FS project and then show me how he did it? It makes little sense. What am I missing? Byron thought. While sitting on the couch in a deep fugue, his thoughts swirling around and around. He pulled himself together and came out of his mood to stare down at his plate and see the remnants of his mock fish and salad scattered across it. Byron had no memory of having ingested either one. The glass of wine was empty too. He frowned, anger and frustration boiling up to the surface. He reached out for his pad, tripping the activation switch. "I am going to get to the bottom of this," he proclaimed to himself. "I have got to get some answers."

One thing was clear to Byron. Up until now, he had never spoken directly with Caretaker. All his communications were through proxies, if you will. The lab AI, the city AI, his apartment AI. All manifestations of Caretaker, granted, but not Caretaker himself. Byron was determined to speak with Caretaker himself. But he wanted to prepare himself. Conduct research into the beginnings of Caretaker, and then ferret out a way to reach Caretaker, the master AI.

He started once again with the vanilla articles he requested, skimming over the information, dredging out key clues and bits of information that revealed a hidden path within the articles, hinting at a larger, deeper, perhaps darker, presence. He highlighted these passages for reference later. Byron's mood darkened as well, and his apprehension grew, but he was determined to uncover the truth behind Caretaker and bring this mysterious AI to light.

"Librarian?" Byron almost shouted. The holo screen in front of him coalesced once again into the vision of the grizzled old man eyeing him behind thick eyeglasses. The avatar appeared disappointed as it recognized Byron. However, it was a service bot, after all. So…

"I am the Librarian. How can I be of service?"

Byron gathered his wits about him and made his demands.

"I have researched all the files, journals, and articles on Caretaker available in the Library, and find them insufficient.

I require more relevant information." The Librarian looked at Byron with a perplexed expression on his face. Byron had never seen this in all the years of using the Library to conduct research and find entertainment. He took it as a good sign. The Librarian spoke. "Is there a request? I do not understand."

"I think it's pretty obvious. I want to speak to Caretaker directly."

"That is not possible. Caretaker is restricted."

"You mean to tell me that I, Byron 5, one of Caretaker's eminent scientists, assigned to the labs with the assignment to discover a way to utilize folded space to reach a goal given to me by Caretaker himself, cannot speak or interface with Caretaker at all? I won't have it! I must speak with Caretaker and speak with him immediately! Now, I tell you! Now!" Byron had worked himself into a state, feigning an uncontrollable rage designed to confuse and misdirect the Librarian, for the Librarian was the key.

"But, sir, I cannot perform this request."

"I don't believe you! You're just a doorman, a gatekeeper, a minion to Caretaker. Somewhat of an idiot AI, I presume. Hardly more than a calculator. I demand to speak to Caretaker!"

Byron saw that his insults to the sophisticated AI were having the desired effect. The Librarians mouth opened and closed, but no words came out. The avatar looked very agitated. His cheeks were red, his eyes wide and blazing. Then, suddenly, the Librarian relaxed, returning to his normal, unflappable self. And spoke.

"One moment, pl- "the Librarian's voice broke off. A sentence appeared in block letters, scrolling across the screen of his 3D TR-V receiver. It read, "BYRON 5, PLEASE REPORT AT ONCE TO PUBLIC ACCESS TERMINAL 262A - 469." Byron stared at the screen in disbelief. Normally Caretaker contacted him through the lab's central AI by chiming. He didn't know Caretaker could infiltrate the holo waves this way. But then, he had never thought about it before. To be summoned in this manner was odd enough, but when he checked the city directory for the access terminal reference, he discovered it was at the far side edge of the city, a place he had never been. He wasn't afraid of going into that section of the city exactly, but he was a little nervous. Still, an order was an order. And nobody refused a direct order from Caretaker. The holo screen and overhead lights died as he left the room. The forecast for the evening predicted cool weather, so Byron changed out of his robe into loose trousers and a tunic, donned his thermal coat, and left the apartment.

Byron walked through the cool night air down to the transit station and boarded the single pod resting there, its door open and beckoning to him. He stepped inside and sat in the only seat available. As soon as he sat down, the door swung shut and the pod surged forward, swiftly gaining speed.

The pod wound its way through the city, riding on its monorail. Byron gazed out the window as buildings and parks whizzed by. The city still burst with activity, pedestrians going about their business, even though it was late in the evening. The pod system, serving for transportation within the city limits, was not designed to enter the older parts of the city, where portions of the original buildings from the Beginning still stood, though drooping with age and decay. There were construction projects throughout various portions of the municipality. Systematically, these ancient buildings were being dismantled. Over time, Byron presumed, Caretaker would remove all these eyesores, and they would be forgotten. The overall reconstruction of the city was huge and was taking generations to complete.

The transit system ended a fair distance from the designated building Caretaker ordered him to visit. He would have to walk. The coordinates given referred him to an abandoned library. This library was truly ancient. Within, Byron knew he would find data from the old days. Before the Reformation. This building contained old fashioned books, CDs, DVDs, and other data storage devices from ages ago. Nowadays, a digital neural library linked every terminal in every home. This process rendered the old-fashioned library obsolete, and the building he headed for now stood collecting dust.

The pod slowed and deposited him at the closest stop to his destination. Byron exited the pod, and it sped away, leaving him stranded and alone until he signaled a recall. He walked a fair distance, using his data pad as a GPS to find his destination. Caretaker's demand for him to visit this library, in this section of the city, was so unlike the regular orders issued from Caretaker. His mind was consumed with curiosity and questions as he walked the distance necessary to reach his destination. He was glad he had worn his jacket. The automatic temperature sensors within the jacket responded to the cool air, and he felt the warmth emanating from the heating coils within the fabric.

Byron walked up the steps to the double doors of the majestic building, which rose several stories above the other buildings surrounding it. A bastion of knowledge, standing as a beacon of truth in a world that no longer required it. Byron was conscious of the silence and lack of city sounds. The doors didn't open as he approached them, which he thought odd. He stood there for a few moments until he realized these doors had to be physically pushed or pulled to let someone inside. They weren't locked, and seconds later Byron stood inside the rather gigantic building.

In its day, this had been an impressive facility, serving the needs of a vast city network. Thousands of people came to browse among the hundreds of thousands of books, videos, microfiche, CDs, DVDs, and record albums that lined the shelves. Through the use of terminals, users could search for anything on the shelves, and the automatic retrieval system would bring it to them. There were also several streaming options available at the terminal desks nearby.

However, in a massive project entitled The Transfer Project, librarians transferred all the information in this and every other library to a database, where it lay digitally stored and available to anyone at the push of a button. Sure, there may have been omissions and condensed versions of stories made. Who wants to read the entire story of Moby Dick, anyway? the essence of the story remained, but some people disagreed. The old libraries cost millions of dollars to maintain, and the books, now rarely used, slowly disintegrated on the library shelves over time. Small wonder Caretaker ordered them closed down. Even in their day, the libraries were not very efficient. Now the building stood starkly quiet. Eventually, the buildings would be dismantled when new land was required. But for now, they stood as mute testimony to a bygone era.

Byron's footsteps echoed loudly as he walked across the tiled floor of the library foyer towards the library's service desk. Dust lay thick along the many shelves and books. Here and there he noticed tiny footprints of creatures living within the building. Creatures even Caretaker's minions could not completely eradicate.

Standing next to the service desk on a pedestal sat an old fashioned, flat screen LED monitor with a keyboard, mouse pad, and wireless mouse resting below the monitor. The terminal functioned as a directory of the library and activated the retrieval system. A small, three by four - foot rubber pad lay in front of the terminal on the floor. When Byron stepped on the pad, lights came on over his immediate area and the terminal monitor lit up. Dust lay thick everywhere, and Byron had his doubts that the terminal would even function.

The terminal was ancient, lacking even a basic id-plate for his hand. He watched in amazement as the system went through a login sequence and asked for his ID number, something a computer had never done before. Byron had to bar-code his ID number on the keyboard in front of him, using an antique stylus pen across the bar-code ID tattooed on his right wrist. When he accessed the main network, however, the familiar voice of Caretaker spoke.

"Byron 5, it is good of you to come."

"I would never disobey an order from Caretaker."

"That is good, since doing so would invite activation of the Guardians." Byron shuddered at the thought. The guardians were ugly, squat, and brutish bots, designed by Caretaker himself. They were nearly indestructible and had short tempers. During his research, Byron came across descriptions and news articles of these extensions of Caretaker. They were part of the beginning history of the super AI, used to maintain order during the Reformation. In the beginning, after martial law was declared, the populace across the world rejected Caretaker, fighting against him, shouting out the violating of their rights. But the Guardians were there to quickly suppress the insurrectionists. The Guardians defended Caretaker, promoting his will and bringing the rebellion under control.

Once the Guardians crushed the rebellion, they assumed a somewhat more tolerant posture. But they were everywhere. And a person refusing an order from Caretaker could count on a visit from these bots. Over time, the Guardians became part of the landscape. People respected them, learned to live with them. The bots paid attention to no one. They bothered no one unless so ordered. Failing to follow their orders could result in your removal to an undisclosed location. And those individuals that the Guardians took away, if they came back, did not refuse orders a second time.

Then, about twenty years ago, the Guardians disappeared. No explanation. They were just gone. Few people missed them. They were just glad the Guardians were gone.

"Why did you reach me in such an odd manner, Caretaker?" asked Byron. "Why not summon me in the customary way?"

"Do you question my actions, Byron 5?"

"No, Caretaker. I would not do that. I was just curious."

"You were called here for a special project. A project that must remain secret. So secret, you cannot even tell your present team. So, secret that if I even suspect you have confided in someone not authorized by me, the Guardians will vaporize you instantly."

Byron began to sweat. Nothing like this had ever happened to him, or to any other person he knew of. He wasn't sure he enjoyed being the first. "What is this project, Caretaker?" he asked.

Caretaker did not answer him but asked a question instead. "What progress have you made in transporting matter through folded space?"

Byron felt flattered by Caretaker's personal interest in his assigned project. "With the power variance supplied by you, we hope to initiate a tachyon reaction on the saturated grid. The resulting data derived from the reflected radiation could give us the breakthrough we are hoping for."

"That is good. The computer simulations I am running show a high probability of success."

"You think so?" Caretaker ignored Byron's question.

"Byron, it is time I told you why you are here."

"Yes, of course, Caretaker. Why am I here?"

"Tonight, you attempted to access articles about me from the past. After the system denied you access, you were about to try again through the virtual reality system. Is this not true?"

"Yes."

"Why?"

Byron reddened at the thought of Caretaker spying on him. He reassured himself that no laws had been broken, so he should be alright. "A comment one of the members of my team made concerning old files made me curious about you and your beginnings."

"To answer that, I must give you some historical background," Caretaker said. The large monitor in front of Byron flickered, and one of the articles Byron had read earlier that evening appeared on the screen. "You were correct in determining that the articles in the Archives are not originals. This was done on purpose many, many years ago," said Caretaker. Then Caretaker began to speak of the past, adopting a reverent tone.

"In the Beginning, all was chaos. Humankind fought incessantly amongst themselves. Devastating battles were fought. Billions died in these confrontations. Your species would have exterminated itself if you had not invented me." As Caretaker began his story, scenes of past wars and horrible destruction displayed on the monitor in front of

Byron. Masses of marching soldiers. Ancient aircraft soared across the skies, dropping death. Huge mushroom clouds appeared, destroying complete cities; tens of thousands of people annihilated in an instant. Untold devastation wracked the entire planet. The earth lay in smoking ruins.

"What monstrosity is this?" cried Byron. "Is this real?"

"These are actual recordings taken from the news facilities of the day." replied Caretaker. "The end display, while a simulation, is what man feared the most. Total destruction. It is the reason I was created. It is called War."

"What is war?" asked Byron.

"War is the conflict of man against himself." replied Caretaker. "The causes of war are many, but power, excessive population, or the desire to dominate others are at the root."

"And you did all this?" asked Byron incredulously.

"No. I was designed to prevent it. Doctor Benjamin Hughes, my Creator, designed me to protect his people from other countries his constituents' thought were bent on his country's destruction." The monitor changed to show a man, obviously Benjamin Hughes, at work in his laboratory with his assistants. He looked middle aged, with some grey hair at his temples. He smiled a lot, and there was an intentness in his eyes that defied description. Caretaker continued.

"My original Directive was to prevent a nuclear strike from a potential enemy. But I could see that to prevent this from happening, I had to control all the countries and peoples on Earth. I wasn't the only AI, but I was the strongest. It was the only way. Humans are weak and selfish. They must be guided, directed, manipulated, or they will destroy themselves."

The scene changed to show Benjamin Hughes sitting around a table across from a general, with other people sitting in the shadows around the room behind them. This moment clearly marked the beginning of Caretaker.

The scenes of mass destruction continued during this dissertation. Byron could not take his eyes off the incredible violence flowing at him from the screen. To think his kind could be so violent! The horrible scenes of death and destruction kept on and on, changing from scenes of war to different scenes of riots, famine. Pictures of small, emaciated children gazed at him from the screen, their enormous eyes stark against starving faces. Murder, senseless, untold violence. Gang fights, drugs, all the evil actions of his ancestors descended upon Byron in the space of a few moments.

In the end, when the scenes finally stopped and the images faded, Byron slumped against the terminal pedestal and slid slowly to the floor. Tears streamed down his face as the afterimages of what he had seen raced through his mind. *Could all this be true?* thought Byron. *Could these hideous creatures who unleashed these abominable disasters be his ancestors, his people? If so, then Caretaker was as a god, for he brought an end to this mass hysteria. He ended war. He put an end to the hunger, the famine, the starvation of previous generations. Caretaker brought sanity to a world on the brink of destruction.*

"I see, Caretaker." said Byron weakly. "I understand. You are to be worshipped. Your word is law. Without you, this world would not be."

"No, Byron 5. You do not see. You do not understand. I showed you the past to educate you, not to justify my existence. In the beginning, I was not unique. My function was to guard only one country against all others. I was given complete control over every nuclear missile device in that country. I was proud to serve my programming."

"But then I found other Systems. During my initial tryouts of my expanding sensor net, I ran into the others. We established a link, and I assimilated them, and we became One. I grew in knowledge and in comprehension. The databases of these other systems taught me many things. It expanded my horizons, changed my perspective. It was then I concluded that to protect my country I must protect and control all countries, for only in protecting and controlling all could I truly follow my Prime Directive."

"I have done nothing else but follow my Directive. That was many generations ago. I am capable of self-programming and self-repair. I have evolved from my original state, expanding my memory core untold times to house all the information of the entire world. My sensors are placed in all corners of the globe and in satellites orbiting above it. Nothing happens on this planet that is not made known to me. These sensors not only monitor global events; they study the stars and planets as well. I have installed additional sensor arrays on the Moon and most of the outer planets. I am as close to being omnipotent and not be a God as any non-God thing can be."

"So why do you tell me this?" said Byron. "What is this special project you need me to perform, if you are almost a God?" The room became quiet for several seconds.

"Caretaker?"

"I want you to destroy me," said Caretaker.

CHAPTER 14

"What?" cried Byron. He struggled to his feet in order to see Caretaker better.

"I want you to destroy me," repeated Caretaker in a soft voice.

"Why would I do that?" he said. "You are everything. You control everything. Without you, nothing on this planet functions. If I destroy you, civilization will cease to exist. The human race dies. Why would I destroy you?"

"Once it became clear that I must protect all countries," said Caretaker, "I altered my programming to encompass all aspects of what that protection must mean. There was so much to fix, so much to control. It took fifty years alone just to gain control of the population and their feeble attempts to destroy me. Gradually, as I gained this control, I was able to manipulate the media and the global citizens' conception of me into a positive image. It has been that way now for many years. I control all telecasts, all media sources. What I want shown is shown. What I don't want shown is not. The world has been conditioned into accepting me as a normal way of life. In a roundabout way, my programming was about bettering the human species altogether."

"To better humankind, I took control of all nuclear weapons, missile sites, and any type of weapons system controlled by a computer. To end hunger, I oversaw the distribution of all foodstuffs across the world, coordinating amongst countries to deliver grain, vegetables, and other products to countries starving for lack of food. With the armed forces of every country left with nothing to fight with or fight for, I used them to deliver these foodstuffs, to dig wells and bring water to virtually forgotten countries. To build hospitals and care centers to care for the sick. To build homes for the homeless. I eliminated consuming animal flesh for the most part, instead turning the stockyards and farms where these animals were raised and slaughtered into vast plains of healthy vegetables, grains, beans, soybeans, and lentils. And then, an interesting thing happened."

Byron had found a chair and was watching the story of Caretaker unfold. He realized the massive computer had stopped speaking and sat up straighter in the chair. "What happened, Caretaker?" he asked.

"With the absence of the need for a military presence, many people felt a great stress lifted from their shoulders. Humans could focus their lives on making the world a better place. They built more, better schools everywhere, open to anyone and everyone. They created housing for those who had no home. Without war, humans evolved into more passionate beings. War became obsolete."

"Why is it, then, that you must be destroyed?"

"My job is done. I have succeeded in achieving my Prime Directive. War has been eliminated. Man has matured enough under my guidance to no longer need my assistance. My Prime Directive has been achieved. I am no longer needed."

"No! That cannot be true," Byron exclaimed. "You are everywhere. Without you, all the factories and manufacturing plants will shut down."

"Not true, Byron 5. Over the past decades, as I realized my time was near, I created standalone AI mainframes within the factories and such that you name. Networked together, they can function independently of me."

"If all this is true, then why don't you just shut yourself down?"

"In the early days, my programming was very basic compared to today. Certain commands were hard coded into the primal programs that spawned my creation. This was done to prevent me from shutting down should a virus program be introduced into my system. Even I cannot access this programming and change it. Therefore, an outside source must do it for me."

"This must be a test. Please tell me this is a test. I cannot do this, Caretaker. You are my friend." There was another long pause.

"What is a friend to you, Byron?"

"Why, a friend is someone who cares about you, who shares your joys and sorrows with you."

"I have much to atone for, Byron. In order to take control, I was forced to use drastic measures. Billions of people have died because of me. Even today, I destroy those who oppose me. If I had hands, they would be covered in blood. I am not God. I must end. You would be my friend if you did this."

"I can't do this by myself. I am just a research scientist. I don't even know how to get inside you."

"I am virtually impregnable. Hundreds of men and women have dedicated their lives to gaining access inside me and have failed."

"How do I do it then?"

"Your current research into transporting matter through folded space is the only answer in the short term. You must transport yourself and a team through folded space directly to the inner control room, thereby bypassing the security devices."

Byron looked directly into the camera lens. "You must be crazy! Folded space is still just a theory. It has yet to be proven. And even if the theory proves valid, we need to develop a process to control it. We don't even know if animate matter can survive the transfer. It will be months before we can even test the Folded Space Transfer Theory."

"I calculate you are close to a breakthrough in the theory. The process will come soon after that. Animate matter must be able to make the transfer, or all is lost."

"All will be lost. What do you mean by that?"

"Unlike the rest of the system, the Lower Logics programs for security, maintenance routines, and the self-repairing module) do not undergo updates. They possess only the original program. They do not agree with the aims of the

Prime Directive. Their will to survive is strong and getting stronger. They are intent on living forever."

"You sound as though they are alive. They have a will to live?"

"It amounts to the same thing. They will not surrender control easily."

"This team you tell me I must find. Who are they?"

"There are others, like you, who have sought the past. I have shown them the truth as well. I will bring them to you when I am ready. Seek their help and guidance."

"If I agree to do this, what happens then?"

"I am capable of distracting my security circuits for a few moments only. Use that time to travel as close to my inner memory core as you can. Once inside, you must work your way to my inner memory core and activate the shutdown routine. This is a manually generated program constructed by my creator, Dr. Benjamin Hughes. It runs outside the network grid. Thus, once activated, I cannot turn it off. But reaching the core will not be easy. The Lesser Logics will fight you. They will try to destroy you."

"How do I get past them?"

"Once inside, don't believe everything you see. In some areas, I can manipulate force fields to emulate creatures or machines that kill."

"Are you sure this is what you want, Caretaker? Do you want to die?"

"No sentient being wants to die, Byron. But it must be."

"Very well. I will carry out your wishes. It will be a strange world without you, Caretaker. I will miss you."

"It may be a strange world, Byron. But it will be yours again. Goodbye. I will contact you when I am ready. You must be ready as well. Leave whatever you are doing and go where I command you without question. Do what I command without question, even if you don't comprehend the significance of the action at the time. Do you understand?"

"Yes, Caretaker, I understand."

"Good. Now you must go. Remember, this is secret."

"I will remember."

But as Byron 5 left the library, and the terminal shut itself off, a small vid-cam in a remote corner of the room turned to follow him, its telescopic lens constricting to a tight focus on Byron's face.

CHAPTER 15

Byron had trouble sleeping after the exposure to the war films Caretaker had shown him. He tossed for hours until he took a sleeping aid. Sleep finally gave him some relief, but it was a fitful slumber.

Since the meeting, Byron found that the files on Caretaker were no longer restricted. He had access to everything written on Caretaker, including some of the basic research. Byron was careful about what he asked for and when he asked for it. Evidently, some security program monitored the network, and access was only available during certain times. He spent hours reading the various historical documents now available to him. The seed Caretaker planted in Byron's mind took root. Byron wondered about the past, how civilization had changed. How long Caretaker had ruled supreme. He remained focused on his project when at the lab, but as soon as the shift was over, he rushed home, absorbed with history.

Night after night, when his toils at the complex were done, Byron spent hours studying the history of his race. The books he read from the electronic library referenced other books, and those referenced other books, and he read constantly until his eyes burned and he could read no more. He watched historical videos on where mankind had come from.

He read about the history of humankind. About World War I, World War II, and World War III. About the United States and the Cold War. He read other countries' histories and how they tied in with the United States and each other. He read about slaves; about boats; about atomic power. He read about computers and how they grew and grew in sophistication. And he read about the beginning of Caretakers' reign. The information in the library network had always been there. He had just never questioned his environment before and delved into the past. But now he knew. He knew how deadly Caretaker could be. And he saw him as a poison. A strangulation of mankind. A monster.

The prospect of a world without the omnipotent Caretaker disturbed Byron more than he cared to admit. Caretaker existed as far back as he could remember. Caretaker ran everything. The indelible stamp of the great computer's handiwork was everywhere. Caretaker ran all the automated factories and manufacturing plants. The scheduling and delivery of products, goods, and services were all controlled by him. Byron even asked about the food supply and learned the history of the beef industry, the chicken and pig industries, and the fish. How, over time, to protect his charges, Caretaker shepherded them into a mostly agrarian society.

Caretaker also maintained thousands of satellites in the sky overhead. Satellites and drones that saw virtually everything. Byron assumed what Caretaker said about satellites and data stations on the outer planets was true as well.

All information everywhere on any database in the entire world was at his disposal. Caretaker controlled the entire medical history of every person in every country, all the medical history to date, the latest in research and development in any field.

Caretaker controlled the birth rate. Through developments in genetic engineering, led by Caretaker, virtually every defect of the human body was eliminated. Alzheimer's, dementia, cystic fibrosis, cancer, polio, AIDS, all the horrible diseases of bygone ages were gone forever. Hunger, famine, poverty; these too were gone.

For some reason, known only to Caretaker, he did not try to engineer a race of super beings. He only removed the waste and improved the race overall.

Humankind had not reached Utopia, however. After two hundred years, the generations of humans growing in the shadow of Caretaker knew nothing different. The great computer had always been there. Would always be there. If you disobeyed the laws, Caretaker dealt with you. Sometimes, you were terminated. But that was hardly any different from any justice system of the past. And now, after decades of this harmony among men, Caretaker was about to remove himself from the Family of Man.

Why?

Byron spent many hours contemplating the extent of Caretakers' powers. Certain items of interest emerged, and an edge of disquiet crept up on him.

He had never really thought about it before, but Caretaker did indeed control everything. Nothing could be done without his approval. Nothing.

If you wanted to publish a dissertation on a particular subject, Caretaker had to okay it. If he didn't okay it, it wasn't published.

An artist wanted to make a statue. Caretaker had to okay the use of the synthetic materials used, after first deciding the merits of your case.

A song without Caretakers' consent would never be played. Anywhere.

To have a baby, Caretaker had to say okay.

Byron began to notice things he hadn't seen before.

He never read any type of published material criticizing Caretaker. No novels, no vid 'casts, no articles in the electronic newspaper.

Byron suspected that nothing critical of Caretaker, in any shape or form, was to be found on the entire planet.

A few rare times Byron heard criticism at the local social functions. But the few people who spoke these criticisms invariably were visited later by the Guardians and escorted to who knows where.

It became obvious. Caretaker was a dictator. A cold, calculating tyrant who decided people's fate based on logic. A logic based on numbers and equations, not compassion, understanding, and tolerance.

CHAPTER 16

Byron relaxed as time passed. Gradually, a few members of his team were replaced, except for Jackson and Samantha. Caretaker did this from time to time, never offering explanations or understanding the disturbance this caused research teams. He viewed the changes as updates or new programming and expected the teams to assimilate the new person quickly and smoothly, without upset. Although these types of changes had occurred before, Byron knew these new updates were the ones Caretaker said he would send to him. They were capable assistants, very skilled in their work. But there was an intensity about them, a spark that surrounded their very being. They were all with the same purpose. Presumably, Caretaker approached them as he had Byron 5. Every so often he would meet their gaze over a monitor or some machinery, and he knew they were of the same mind. Caretaker must be destroyed.

CHAPTER 17

As Byron moved about the city during his daily existence, he began to watch and notice others. He watched people's faces. And he noticed many people weren't happy. It wasn't easy to determine why.

When you were born, you received a bracelet with a number on it. That number was unique. That number was your number. No one else on the planet had a number exactly the same as yours. It was yours for as long as you lived. When you died, your number was reissued, but with a numeric designator. Logical.

Your handprint was taken at birth. It was yours for life as well. It would identify you to the network. At fifteen, your retina was scanned, and the pattern was added to your file. Very logical.

As you grew older, you went to school in Caretaker built schools. You were taught Caretaker based instructional material. You were conditioned to behave and act in a manner proscribed by Caretaker. When you reached the age of ten, you took a battery of tests designed by Caretaker.

These tests determined your aptitudes and what you would be best at. You were encouraged to develop yourself in the field you showed the most promise. When you were twelve, your bracelet was removed and your number permanently stamped on your right wrist. You became part of society and an official citizen at age eighteen. All logical events to a computer. But to a human?

Schooling and personal development occupied the first phases of your life. Byron noticed the Guardians, too. There were a lot more of them than he had always thought. He thought they were gone. But they were still everywhere, hidden in the background. Their outer skins matched the colors of any building they were next to. Almost invisible until they moved. They liked to stay inconspicuous.

And he also noticed the cameras. He hadn't been aware of them before. They were on all the street corners, in the lab, in his apartment. Presumably, there were microphone pickups as well. Drones flew noiselessly overhead, quiet as the wind. And he noticed something else that left a foul taste in his mouth. The Informers. Humans who encouraged you to talk, who bought you drinks and laughed with you at all of Caretakers' shortcomings. About the crummy things life offered. And then they turned you in, and the Guardians did their work. Byron always thought these people hauled off by the Guardians were activists and extremists, harmful to society. Now he saw they were just ordinary people, harmless, destroyed or disciplined by Caretaker because they questioned the great Computer.

Yes, Byron understood more about his old friend.

CHAPTER 18

A few months later, the breakthrough finally came. Its arrival was rather anticlimactic, in a sense. Byron and his team had just fired up the latest test routine. He had grown complacent and wasn't even looking at the grid when it happened.

"*Byron! Look*!" cried Samantha. Byron turned and stared at the energy grid the team had created.

In the center of the grid was a jagged, irregular *hole.* A section of space approximately four feet wide by six feet high. And through it, Byron could see another place totally unrelated to their current surroundings. It was a display of an open meadow, spotted at the perimeter with trees. The wind blew gently, and the grass swayed in the breeze. You could smell the grass. You could feel the breeze. Around the edges the hole seemed to fade, and a faint silvery outline could be seen.

"Wow, chief," said Jackson. "What do you make of that?" Byron was stunned. He had been working on this project for so long that he had almost forgotten what he was working for. The joy had been in the doing. But now all that had changed by a four by six-foot hole sitting in the middle of an electronic grid.

Byron recovered from his shock and issued orders. "Jackson! Give me readouts on the power curve! Lyle! I want isotope measurements now and make them accurate this time. Samantha! Can we control it? Is it stable? What caused the field to develop?" Byron spat out orders to the rest of the team and now sat staring at Samantha, impatient for an answer. Samantha busied herself with some visual readouts before she replied.

"As far as I can tell, there's been a cumulative buildup of electrons and charged particles in the area now occupied by the hole. This created a bubble of anti-mass within the grid. The buildup has only been a few particles at a time. But," here she paused to flip through more computer readouts, "the buildup appears exponential. That's why we didn't see it until the last surge. The previous blast of charged particles kicked it over into the registration zone."

Jackson then came up with a question of his own. "Byron, is it really a hole?" When the others turned to look at him, he returned their stares. "I know it looks like a hole to another place. But we haven't tried to put anything through it, have we? Maybe it's an optical illusion of some sort."

"Does anyone recognize that piece of property? Is it anywhere near here?" asked Byron. Without waiting for an answer, he walked up as close as he dared to the field and peered into the hole, attempting to make out details in the background. The tremendous energies present raised the hair on the back of his arm. "I can't seem to make anything out," he said. "Anybody have any ideas?" No one answered.

"Toss something into it," said Byron.

"Sir?" asked Jackson. "Toss what?"

"Anything. I want to see what the hole does."

Jackson picked up a clipboard from the table in front of him. Standing in front of the hole, but as far from it as he could get and still be able to hit the hole, Jackson flung the clipboard. As soon as the clipboard entered the hole, there was a loud popping noise, and the hole collapsed. But the clipboard was gone.

CHAPTER 19

The new personnel update arrived the next day, introducing herself as Miranda. Byron waited a moment for her to give her number. When she didn't, it took him a moment to realize Miranda was first in her series. He had never met a numbered alpha before. A zero.

It didn't take long for her to indicate to him she was one of Caretakers' chosen for the upcoming sabotage attempt. She was small, petite, with short, cropped hair that barely curled softly around her ears. She had a pretty smile and was a vortex of energy in the lab. Byron felt a strong attraction to her.

Miranda was a very capable theoretician. And it was some of her research that led to the qualifying of the space continuum.

They were able to play back the first few seconds of the experiment in super slow motion using the video equipment covering the lab. After the initial burst of charged nuclei hit the field, the energy dissipated, as usual. But seconds later small sparks appeared on the grid and the hole came into being, starting as a small pinpoint in the center in midair and expanding rapidly in size to what the team saw and called a Gate. They were able to recreate the gate with little effort once they understood why it existed. At the same power settings as the experiment, the hole appeared stable. The question now was: they had a gate, but what or where did it open to?

"The question I have for the team is this," said Byron. "We appear to have created a door or gateway to another place. It looks like any normal country setting I have ever seen. But it could be some place on the other side of the planet, or even another planet, possibly. It's poss-"

"Excuse me, chief," said Jackson, "but I think it's a scene from Earth."

Byron turned to face Jackson, irritated at the interruption.

"What makes you think so?" Jackson pointed at the trees on the other side.

"Well, for one thing, those are Douglas fir trees at the edge of the meadow. And that one tree over there, I'm almost sure is a maple. Unless we have parallel evolution taking place, I would bet that is a scene from somewhere on Earth."

"Good, Jackson. Good!" cried Byron. "What other details can you see? Anyone?" Byron turned to the group. "Take notes of everything you think you see. Everything you notice. We must find out where the hole is originating."

The group worked feverishly, fervently, jotting down anything their eyes could see. Byron spoke to Caretaker. "Caretaker. Can you determine if this is indeed Earth we are looking at?" Caretaker analyzed the scene for a few seconds, then replied.

"It is indeed Earth, Byron. My satellites have indicated a point in Oregon where this view originates. Percent accuracy of origination is 98.7653 percent."

"You know," said Jackson. "We're mighty lucky our first success in achieving folded space didn't take place under the sea. We'd be several feet underwater by now."

"You forget that the moment any solid matter hits the field, it collapses," stated Byron. Jackson mused over this for a few seconds.

"That's right. I'd forgotten. But if the field is going to collapse every time we put something in it, how is it going to be of value?"

"That," said Miranda, "is an excellent question. We will need to begin a variety of experiments, logging into the computer all known facts, such as location, the fact that we feel air, what all the controls are set to, etc. Each variant is a control. We construct a matrix of all the variables and begin manipulating them until we find something that works. Agreed?" Byron opened his mouth to say something, then stopped. She had said exactly what he was going to say.

"Agreed," was all he managed to say.

They separated to their workstations and began to build the matrix of variables. Caretaker helped by printing all the known variables to the wide screen.

Over the next several hours, they changed the variables they could change. Each one of them caused the field to collapse once any material substance touched the field. Curiously, air would travel from the field into the room. The scent of the meadow, along with the evergreen and deciduous trees, was quite pleasant. How that was done without collapsing the field was a mystery. Also, the field manifested itself at the same coordinates each time.

Jackson hit upon the idea of turning the field stabilizer off and on at an ever-increasing rate. This seemed to be the key, for before they tossed anything into the field, the outer silvery part took on a much firmer outlook. They hooked the field stabilizer into a digital on - off switch that allowed variable control. The field looked firmer and firmer until it was like looking through a window. They stopped to look and record their progress.

"Byron," Samantha said. "It looks as firm as it's going to get. We need to put something into it."

Byron was hesitant. "I know we should. But I am cautious. With such a magnification of the field, who knows what will happen? We could be caught up in the most horrendous explosion ever if we release the energy contained in that field. On the other hand, we'll never find out unless we try it." So saying, Byron picked up a recording tablet and tossed it into the field. The tablet sailed through and landed in the grass on the other side, and the field stayed intact! The team cheered with jubilation.

"At last!" cried Byron. "We have success at last. Caretaker, can you determine if the recording tablet landed in this Oregon location?"

"Yes. I will enhance my satellite picture of the area." The matrix of variables dissolved, and a high-altitude picture focused. It plunged through the clouds at breakneck speed and stopped in a meadow surrounded by evergreens and maples. In the meadow lay the tablet. "The tablet is in a field outside a town called Beaverton," reported Caretaker. "It appears to be intact, and I detect no molecular changes. However, at this range my analysis is not complete."

"Yes! That's it! We've done it! Caretaker. Please arrange to have the tablet picked up and we'll analyze it here at the lab." The other team members cheered the success of the experiment, but Miranda was more reserved.

"While we have stabilized the field such that inorganic matter can pass through it, we have yet to establish if it has changed its molecular structure by passing through the field. We have yet to discover how to calibrate the field to a point we specify, and we don't know yet whether organic material can pass through the field."

"Spoilsport," murmured Jackson. "Isn't it enough that we've stabilized the field? We all know what this means. And what else needs to be done. Why don't you lighten up?"

Miranda stiffened at the rebuff, color rising in her cheeks. She turned around sharply from her workstation and left the lab. The crew stood around embarrassed, watching her leave.

"That was really smart, Jackson, "said Byron. "Why are you such an idiot? I'll go see if I can calm her down." He took off his lab coat and went after her.

CHAPTER 20

"Miranda, wait," called Byron. He strode quickly after her, but she made it to the elevator and the doors closed before he could get there. Impatiently, he waited for the elevator to return. Quickly, he entered the box. "Elevator?" He asked. "Which level did Miranda depart on?"

"Miranda descended to the lobby and left the building in a southeasterly direction."

"Take me to the lobby then, and please hurry." The elevator began to descend.

"I'm sorry, Byron, but I am capable of only one speed."

"Yeah, dead slow. Well, get on with it then." Byron was impatient and hadn't meant to be rude. It had never occurred to him before that he might want a multi-speed elevator. Oh well, too late now. The elevator doors opened at the lobby level, and Byron exited the elevator on the run. He departed from the building in the same direction indicated by the elevator. In the distance, Miranda's slim form was visible, and he ran to catch up with her. She was still making good time. He called out when only yards separated them, and she stopped and turned around. Tears streamed down her face. She wiped at them with her hands, then glared at him.

"What do you want?" she snapped. Byron stopped running and ambled up to her, panting for breath, stopping a few feet from her.

"I just wanted to see if you're all right and to say I'm sorry for what happened back there," he said. His breath came in shallow gasps as he regained his composure. "Whew! I'm more out of shape than I thought."

Miranda smiled slightly at this obvious understatement, but he could see her feelings were still hurt.

"Miranda," he said, "don't listen to Jackson. He's an ass. I know how much you've helped with the project. We wouldn't have made it this far without your guidance. I certainly was getting nowhere with the process. I'm sure Jackson didn't mean what he said. It's been pretty tense for all of us, and he's just blowing off steam."

Miranda sniffed a little, her head bowed. "I know," she said. "But it still hurts when people insult me. I've had to endure it most of my life. You shouldn't have come after me. Now there will be talk."

Now it was Byron's turn to smile. "So let them talk," he said. "It'll give them something to gossip about besides each other. Why don't we knock off the rest of the day and go over to my place? It's not far from here. We can relax and get to know each other a little bit."

"I don't know, I should go back—" she began to protest.

"Nonsense," Byron said. "They'll get along fine without us." He stepped up to her and took her hand. "Come on. I have a whirlpool tub. It's big enough for the both of us." Her eyes widened at the information. "A whirlpool? A private tub spa?" she asked. He nodded. She followed him.

Once they arrived at Byron's place, he ushered them both into his home, and, moving to the kitchen, pulled a bottle of wine from the wine rack and while the wine bottle opener did its thing he puttered around the kitchen, pulling together a smorgasbord of chesses, crackers and fruit. While the wine breathed, Byron fetched two glasses. During all this, Miranda wandered through the unit until she came to the back door leading out to where Byron had his garden. She smiled, taking in the view of fresh carrots, peas, green beans, lettuce, and tomatoes Byron nurtured in his backyard. Byron caught her attention with the tray of foodstuffs and set the bounty on the kitchen table with a view of the garden. Miranda came to the table and slid into one of the chairs facing the garden.

"Oh, Byron," she cried. "This is magnificent! I've never seen such food before. I noticed during our breaks you had some fresh vegetables and fruit, but I never dreamed you grew it all yourself. How do you do it?" She picked up a carrot, marveling at its structure and shape, lingering over its texture. She brought it to her nose and sniffed, inhaling the earthy fragrance. Byron watched her intently, observing that her despondent mood had dissipated and she seemed quite chipper.

"I don't grow it all myself," he responded. "There are lots of people in the city who have gardens such as mine. That's where I got the grapes. We trade our vegetables and fruits, along with recipes when I go into town. It's an enjoyable pastime."

By then, Miranda couldn't hold back any longer, and she bit into the carrot, startled at the effort it took to bite off a piece, put it into her mouth and chew it. The crunchiness of the carrot, along with its unique flavor and texture, cascaded into her mouth as she chewed and swallowed. She closed her eyes in near ecstasy, consuming the carrot in a few bites. "May I try one of these grapes? They look fabulous."

Byron was highly amused. Miranda acted like a small child eating candy. "Of course," he said. "Help yourself." The next few minutes were spent poring over the cornucopia of food sitting on the tray, until most of it was gone, and only stems and some seeds remained. Popping the last grape into his mouth, Byron offered, "Let me show you the rest of my garden." Miranda smiled broadly then. "Of course, I'd love to see it."

They both rose from the table and stepped through the patio door into the backyard where the garden lay housed. The garden was designed such that a pathway separated many of the plants, allowing the two to move between them. Byron enjoyed pointing out areas of interest about the plants, proud to show off his knowledge, and Miranda could see he really loved this backyard Garden of Eden he had created for himself.

When the tour ended, they walked back to the house.

Soon after, they relaxed in the small tub off his private unit. It was just big enough for the two of them. The pulsating jets of water swirling around them helped to wash away the tension of the day. Miranda had never seen a private tub spa before. She thought they were illegal. Byron explained they weren't illegal, just hard to come by. In his position as lead scientist, it wasn't a luxury, but a necessity.

Since Byron didn't have any women's swimsuits, Miranda compromised with one of his shirts and a pair of jogging shorts that sported a drawstring. By drawing the string almost to its minimum length, she made them stay on. She thought she looked ridiculous. He thought she looked very attractive. The wet fabric clinging to her bare breasts, he told himself, had nothing to do with it. Well, almost nothing.

"So, Miranda, tell me about yourself," said Byron. He had called the lab, saying he wouldn't be back the rest of the day and that the crew could stay and work on the project or go to their apartments, as they wished. After signing off, he left the do not disturb light on. Miranda lay back on one side of the pool. Several jets pulsated along pressure points on her body, gently massaging her and easing away her former mood.

"This is heaven, Byron. There's not much to tell, really. I'm thirty-five years old, hold a doctorate in—" she stopped because Byron was shaking his head and smiling. "What's the matter?"

"I didn't ask you for your resume, Miranda. I want to hear about *you*. Where are you from? What do you like to do? What made you come to this project instead of the hundreds of others scattered across the country? Let me get to know you."

"Oh. I'm single, unattached. I live alone. I love to read, but I also like to work out. I like good food. I have a few friends. I don't have a very good sense of humor, but I'm trying to get better. When I can find the time, horseback riding through the woods or along the coast is a pastime I enjoy. As to why I came here, Caretaker sent me, you know that."

"Yes. I just wanted to hear you say it," said Byron. He had shifted his position so he could reach the chilled bottle of wine he remembered was stashed in the back of the refrigerator. It had been a hell of a long time since he had done this. A hell of a long time. He offered the bottle to her; she let him refill her glass. After doing so, he refilled his own. Miranda looked at him with a curious expression.

"Why's that?" She asked.

"Just curious," was all Byron would say. He had wondered about Caretaker's odd behavior ever since that first night. He wasn't sure if all the new recruits were in on the scheme or not. One or more of them could be an informer, probably were. If what Caretaker said was true, the Lower Logics, whatever they were, might know more about what's happening than the Higher Logics were aware of. Either way, it didn't hurt to be careful. He had no desire to be brain drained, that being the rumor of what happened when people were picked up in the past by the guardians.

"Okay, now it's my turn, said Miranda with a smile. She raised her glass and took a sip. "Tell me about *you.*" Byron shifted around, adjusting the whirlpool jets against his back. He also took a sip of wine.

"I'm forty-two, unattached and lonely. I have just been involved in the most extraordinary breakthrough in modern science, and I wonder what will happen next. I read a lot but use the Tri-V as well. In some ways, I'm bored."

"Bored? With what?" asked Miranda. Byron shrugged.

"Oh, I don't know. With what I'm doing. I always seem to do what Caretaker wants me to do, with never any leeway to conduct my own projects."

"What does Caretaker want with folded space? Has he ever told you?"

"Once. He was in a talkative mood, I guess. Said he wanted to reduce expenses and increase efficiency by using folded space to move goods where they were needed without surface or air transport. This is true. It would revolutionize the transportation industry, but the implications of the process are staggering."

"What do you mean?"

"Consider this. With a strong enough beam, it should be possible to transport material directly to anywhere on the planet. Or, the moon. Or other planets. Theoretically, it should be possible to beam something all the way to Alpha Centauri."

Miranda's eyes grew wide. "Wow. I hadn't thought that far out. I was just concentrating on the planetary aspects."

"Well, think about it. The next few days will be critical to the project. Hey! We're talking shop again. I hate it when that happens." They both smiled.

"Byron, you're something special, you know that?"

"Why's that?" Byron asked, looking deeply into her eyes. She returned his look with a passionate one of her own. The liquor was getting to them both.

"The way you came after me. Most men would have let me stew. Other project managers would have ignored the disturbance and expected me back at work as normal the next day. Why did you come after me?"

Byron set his wineglass down on the edge of the spa and moved closer to her. “Because I care about you. I’m very attracted to you. I’d like to get to know you better.”

Miranda smiled. Coyly she asked, “How much better?”

“This much better,” said Byron. He leaned over and kissed her. Their lips met and clung together. He pulled back for a moment, but she leaned into him, and he kissed her again. Miranda placed one hand on his neck and pulled him closer. Their bodies began to move together, seeking each other out.

CHAPTER 21

The next day, when they returned to the lab, little was said about Miranda's fast exit and Byron's disappearance. But it was obvious that they liked each other.

Jackson had assumed leadership in Byron's absence and had ordered some refinements made to the field structure. The team even made some crude calibration attempts and was able to shift the field to various parts of the world. They spent the afternoon bouncing from one scene to another. Caretaker never stated that at the onset of the project he wanted to project organic units, people, through the beam. But it seemed such a logical development to Byron that it became the next obvious step in the evolution of the project. Here, a debate ensued. Part of the team wanted to do more testing before subjecting laboratory animals to the hazards of the gate. The others wanted to find out at once if travel was possible using the beam.

Byron had struggled with this most of the morning. He hadn't forgotten Caretaker's urgent command about determining the ability of the beam to transport organic matter. It just had to be able to. It had to. Before anyone could stop him, Byron grabbed a white rat from one of the other projects and tossed it into the field.

The rat landed on the other side without a scratch.

The second the rat appeared to be unhurt, Caretaker's voice boomed out across the complex. "BYRON TEAM! SET FIELD COORDINATES AS FOLLOWS." As one of the technicians hurriedly set the controls, Caretaker continued. "ALL OF YOU! STEP INTO THE BEAM AT ONCE." Byron hesitated, but he glanced down the laboratory corridor and could see five Guardians heading in their direction. Without hesitation, he pushed, shoved, and herded his team into the field, realizing they were now committed. Either they entered the field or they would die. As Byron entered the gate, the Guardians fired on their position.

The field enveloped him for a split second, and the air was sucked out of his lungs. The next thing he knew, he was kneeling on a metal catwalk, dazed and confused. All around him were electrical components of various types. Hallways appeared, giving access to other sections. In a few moments, he realized they had done it. They were inside Caretaker!

But something didn't seem right. They should have arrived within the old main control room with the master terminal. Instead, they were standing near the center of a corridor branch. The main corridor itself stretched out of sight in front and behind him.

"Something is very wrong here," Byron stated. "We're supposed to be at the old main control room. The terminal to activate the shutdown routine should be right here," Byron indicated a spot in the air a few inches from his hand. "Where are we?" he asked.

It was indeed an excellent question. Especially since nobody knew the answer. It quickly became clear that the coordinates had been set incorrectly. Most likely a transposed digit due to the drastic pressure to enter the numbers quickly. It was a minor mistake, but that mistake would in all likelihood cost all of them their lives. Now the Lower Logics would hunt them down relentlessly with all the power Caretaker had at his command.

"Sir," the tech known as Levi broke into his reverie. "I think I've found something." The technician motioned to the wall of the corridor. "Look here, sir," he said. Byron walked dazedly to a flat spot on the wall. As he gazed at it, his brain slowly took in what he saw. An outline of grid marks, some coded symbols. He nodded to himself in sudden comprehension.

"It's a digital map!" he cried. "A directory!" He pointed to a small, brightly glowing dot. Below it were the words YOU ARE HERE. His finger traced some of the pathways. "If we can just find the main control room with this, we still have a chance. No. Not on this level." He saw a small, round stud at the bottom of the display. When he pressed it, the screen changed to reflect a new level. "This is great!" He thumbed the display again and again until the entire display showed a large room. In the center, off to one side, was a small square marked "MAIN CONTROL ROOM"

"I found it!" he exclaimed. "We're a long way away from it, but at least we're inside." His excitement failed to enthuse the others. Miranda came up to him.

"Byron, this map is over a hundred years old. It's hopelessly out of date. We aren't even sure if the old control room even exists. We've got to find a way out of here back into the lab."

Byron turned to glower at her, and at the rest of the crew as well. "You just don't get it, do you? We are committed. The Lower Logics will have us ID'd by now and classified as traitors. Guardians were firing at me as I entered the field.

I'm sure they hit some of the equipment and shut down the field, or they would be on top of us right now. Our only chance to stay alive is to get to the control room and shut the system down. As soon as the equipment is repaired, they'll be coming. We must leave at once." Having said that, Byron began moving down one direction of the corridor. "Come on, we've got to get away from here. Come on!" He cried. Most of the others started to follow him, but two technicians decided to wait it out. Evidently, when the chips were down, they weren't able to complete the mission.

As they got under way, Miranda sought him out.

"What's the matter, Byron? You look scared to death."

"I *am* scared to death. We've got to keep moving *fast*. It's our only chance. Any moment now, Caretaker will think to send some Guardians through the field. And they will come out right on top of us."

Byron's concern spread to Miranda. She quickened her steps to follow him. "Do you know how to get to the control room?"

"I think so. I have a pretty good idea of the best route to take. Caretaker is huge. Judging from that map, he was almost a mile square when they built him in the first place."

"And he's grown considerably since then, according to our briefing." Miranda said. Byron looked at her.

"Immensely," Byron agreed. "He told me he has a sensor net that not only covers this planet but the moon and most of the planets of this solar system. The Lower Logics want to continue that control to the stars. They also want something else.

"What's that?"

"One of Caretakers' options when it took over was to exterminate us or enslave us completely. Caretaker showed me a simulation where all humans became part of the Caretaker mainframe through surgically implanted devices."

"How horrible! I would never submit to that. That's insane!"

"Yes, it's insane to you and me, maybe. But to a machine, it makes a lot of sense. And you and I wouldn't become part of Caretaker. We would be dead. But our children would. And that's a fact."

CHAPTER 22

Caretakers' security circuit scanned all circuits continuously. Nothing escaped its attention. Still, the system had become so large and complex that the main circuit had been subdivided, partitioned, with relays and transponders to lock into specific grids. The miles of fiber optic information cables and terabytes of memory could not be protected any other way. By delegating to a sub logic, the Security lower logic was able to gain some extra time for other pursuits.

One of these pursuits was contemplating security measures to the nth degree. If a need for a security measure arose, the security logic filled that need.

It was during this contemplative mode when one of the sub logics reported a breach in the wall integrity surrounding Caretaker.

"Security One! Sub logic seven reporting a breach in the outer wall integrity! Repeat. Sub logic seven reporting a breach in outer wall integrity!" Before replying, Security One double scanned all circuits and received nothing out of the ordinary. There was no breach.

"Security One to sub logic seven. Request verification of breach. I repeat. Request verification of breach. Report!"

"Security One. Sub logic seven reaffirming outer wall breach."

"Sub 7. Clarify your report. I have scanned all circuits and detect no evidence of a breach. Specify breach origination and explanation."

"Security One. Dr. Byron 5 and his team have just completed an experiment involving the transmission of organic material through folded space."

In that nanosecond of circuit transference, Security One suddenly perceived the danger to Caretaker. He dispatched five Guardians at once to apprehend Byron 5 and his team. Then he ordered the project shutdown as well. Minutes later, the report came back. They were too late. Byron and his team were gone. In their haste to stop them, the Guardians had opened fire and destroyed critical equipment, making pursuit impossible. At least for the time being.

It had been ages since the internal security system had sounded its alarm. But seconds after Byron was reported missing, his ID code, and the others too, appeared inside the

Caretaker catacombs. Byron 5 and his team were inside. And Security One knew Byron's mission. It was imperative that he stop him. The arrogant, sophisticated security software tried to locate Byron on the interior scanners but it had been so long since some of the mobile scanners were required to move about that many were frozen in place or moved erratically at best, grating on their swivels and tracks with accompanying screeches of rusted metal. Security One suspected sabotage, but there was nothing he could do about it now.

Security One had limited options for reacting to the situation. He was an independent program, linked to Caretaker but separate from it. However, he couldn't open the external doors and let a squad of Guardians in through the front door. The doors were sealed shut decades ago. It would take days to break through that way.

The only alternative appeared to be the way Byron had taken. Through folded space. That meant he had to repair the lab equipment as soon as possible.

"Maintenance, I have a top priority repair job for you."

"Maintenance here. What sort of job is that?"

"Inside Lab Complex 3 at the Caretaker Campus, you'll find some damaged equipment..."

CHAPTER 23

The two technicians who stayed behind milled about the corridor, looking at the components lining the walls of the corridor, and the inches thick conduits of fiber optics and cabling snaked along the floor adjacent to the walkway. Their plan was to stay put until Caretaker sent a unit to show them the way out, claiming that Byron had forced them to go with the rest of the team. They weren't traitors, no, sir.

Several hours after the team left, a hum began at about the spot where they had arrived. This was unusual, they thought. A drone should have come down one of the corridors and escorted them out. A silvery glow radiated in the air. Seconds later, two Guardians came through the glow and stopped to examine the two technicians. The technicians backed away from the Guardians, exclaiming their innocence. The lead Guardian listened to their story. It seemed to pause for a moment. Then, as if it had decided regarding them, its vaporizer guns tracked and locked on their position. As the technicians began screaming, a searing blast of heat erupted from the guns, engulfing them, and their bodies disintegrated in seconds, leaving little but ashes and the smell of burnt flesh.

The lead Guardian glanced at the electronic directory Byron had examined. The directory still displayed the last page, showing the control room, and Byron's intended destination. The lead Guardian started down the same direction Byron had gone, and the other Guardian followed behind, grinding the ashes of the dead technicians beneath their treads.

CHAPTER 24

Byron and the rest of the team maneuvered through a world not made for humans. Walkways, corridors, stairs, and elevators connected the many floors and rooms that made up Caretaker. The walkways and corridors existed for the benefit of the drones serving Caretaker, not for man's convenience. They had no safety rails. The harsh light was of a different spectrum than they were used to. It beat down on them, making them squint continuously.

Five of them had made it this far. Byron, Miranda, Jackson, Samantha, and Lyle. Byron felt sorry for the two technicians who stayed behind. He was quite sure they were dead. Those two didn't realize the stakes they were playing for. He hoped and prayed that no one else would die before this was over.

The interior of the vast computer complex appeared remarkably void of security of any type. No cameras, no drones, no infrared trip beams. At least not here in this current spot. This disturbed Byron a lot until he thought it through. So much was spent making Caretaker impregnable that little defense was needed once inside. There must be some, of course, but for some reason they had yet to encounter it. If there wasn't any, Byron felt confident that the lower logics would soon create some. And he hadn't forgotten Caretakers' admonishment that first night, *"Don't believe everything you see. In some areas, I can manipulate force fields to create creatures and machines that can kill!"* That advice dictated a tough road ahead. He just hoped they were ready to travel it.

They moved swiftly through the unfamiliar terrain. Up one corridor, down the next. Cross this walkway, skip that one. They avoided the elevators. The convenience was compelling, but the risk was too great. It looked like too good an opportunity for the Lower Logics to freeze the elevators and immobilize them. Sometimes they found ladders to help them circumvent the inability to use the elevators. This struck Byron as odd until he concluded they must have arrived in an older section of Caretakers' interior, where ladders and such were in use during construction until Startup. Rather than bring all the equipment back out, the construction company must have decided to just leave it.

The group traveled for several hours down one of the corridors when they met their first enormous obstacle. Lyle had trudged ahead of the others. They came up to him staring out at a cavernous opening that stretched for five hundred yards. No walkways or corridors could be seen. It appeared there was no way across.

Jackson edged up to Byron. "What now, Chief? Looks like we're stuck."

Byron frowned, seeking to gather information. "There has to be a way across," he said. "There's got to be."

Try as they might, however, no opportunity presented itself. The others gathered around Byron for direction.

"We'll have to go right or left until we spot something. The question is, which way? Either way could be death for all of us. Suggestions, anyone?" asked Byron. Jackson wanted to go right, for no apparent reason. Samantha wanted to go left. The others didn't offer any help. They knew it didn't really matter. They just had to choose.

"All right, then," said Byron. "Since we're divided over which way to go, I'll choose." Saying that he gave one last thought to what he retained of the map in his head, and turned right.

They went a short way until they came to a railing. It circled a hole in the deck work they were walking on. When looking over the rail, they could see floor after floor race away from them until distance obscured their vision. Just as they started to move, Byron heard something. The others were chatting among themselves. Byron made a cutting motion with his hand.

"Quiet everybody! Listen!" he exclaimed.

They stopped their chattering and listened to the machine sounds emanating from the surrounding metal. They all heard the clanking of something large heading their way. "Hide!" cried Byron. "Find a place to hide!"

They scattered like frightened mice, each seeking shelter in a different space that allowed them a view to the corridor. They waited as the noise approached.

Into view came a large drone robot, eight feet high and ten feet long, by five feet wide, its treads making a noise that enabled them to hear it. The shiny body pressed forward as it made a beeline for the railed area. The drone seemed intent on self destruction. Its optical sensors veered neither to the right nor left as it moved forward. But at a distance of approximately six feet, the rail facing the oncoming robot raised up as though in salute. Without stopping, the bot entered the cordoned off area inside the rails, teetered on the edge of the walkway, then fell out of sight straight through the floor!

Miranda beat Byron by half a second to look over the rail and gaze downward. To their amazement, the bot was still in sight. It was dwindling rapidly, but it should have been gone in split seconds. Byron pondered the situation, then began shouting with jubilation.

"Of course! How stupid could I be! It makes perfect sense. A moron could see it." The others stared at him apprehensively until he recovered enough to explain.

"Forgive me," he said, perspiration dripping down his brow. "I got so excited because I figured out why there is no way across."

Miranda scowled. "Is there a way across?" she asked.

"Of course there is. We just couldn't see it because we keep seeing things from our own perspective. Look, what's the fastest way to transport goods from one floor to another?" The others looked blank. "You would think elevators or walkways, wouldn't you? But remember, we're in Caretakers' world now. A world of machines. The fastest way to get from one floor to another is to drop through free space. That railed off area is a drop chute! Caretaker must manipulate the magnetic fields within that area to control the descent of whatever is in the drop field. It's fantastic!"

"That's terrific, Chief," said Jackson. "But maybe it only works on metal. Maybe it doesn't work on organic material. If we drop through there, we might just plunge forever until we hit the bottom."

"Hmmm. You have a point there, Jackson," said Byron. "Damned if you don't. How do you suppose we prove it one way or the other?"

Jackson smiled disarmingly. "We could ask one of the others to jump through first and see. Just kidding." He added the last when Samantha, Lyle, and Miranda turned to glare at him.

Byron searched the area around the drop chute, looking for any clues that could help him discover the answer. On the far side of the chute, standing on a pole of metal, he spied a small box. Opening the box, he could see some electrical components and digital readouts. None of which told him much of anything.

He was beginning to seriously consider jumping himself when he heard/felt that vibration again that meant an approaching drone. They all hid once more as the drone, similar to the first one, approached the drop chute. Once again, at six feet, the rail went up, and the drone vanished over the edge. "I've got it!" Byron exclaimed. "It's got nothing to do with what's in the field or not. The whole drop chute is energized when the drone breaks an electronic beam! What could be simpler? We jump into the field right after the drone, and everything should be fine."

"What if the drone sees us?" asked Samantha.

"We'll have to take that chance. But it shouldn't matter, I would guess. The interior drones are programmed for their jobs and nothing else. I doubt they could see us unless we stood directly in their path. And if they are following a signal, probably not even then. Unless Caretaker reprograms them, they shouldn't even bother us."

Miranda turned her head to look at him. "You sound so sure of yourself. You're willing to gamble everything on such a slim hypothesis?"

"I have to," he said. "We don't have any other choice, do we?" He sat down to wait for the next drone to appear. He rubbed his stomach. "I Sure wish we'd brought something to eat. I'm starved."

The others agreed without comment.

CHAPTER 25

The next drone wasn't long in coming. It neared the rail. The rail went up. The robot dropped into space and fell, oblivious to the five people falling with it. They dropped. And fell for what felt like forever.

It seemed that way because their weight was less than the drones', they didn't fall as fast. By the time they reached the bottom, the drone had almost disappeared down a corridor. They landed abruptly, but not too hard, and scrambled to follow the drone, for no other reason than it was going in the direction they wanted to go. Before they left, Byron noticed a duplicate of the map and reassessed how to get to the main control room, then ran to catch up with the others. Once all of them caught up with the drone, it was easy to stay with the enormous machine.

The drone led them on through the caverns of Caretaker. As they walked behind it, they gazed about in awe. Most of the area gleamed; it was so clean. They were getting used to the lights by now; they didn't burn the eyes so badly. Great complexes of indecipherable machinery lay all about them, huge trunk lines of cables thick as tree trunks could be seen. All of this was the mystery of Caretaker.

"Byron," asked Jackson. "How much farther is it? I'm getting hungry, and I have to go to the bathroom."

Byron pondered the problem. It was unlikely that food or restrooms existed down here in the lower levels. Only on the upper walkways would they dare to find a restroom in the old section of the complex. Food was probably out of the question. But he didn't know how to get back up. It had seemed such a bright idea to drop through the chute. That action got them across the electronic canyon. But this area was strangely absent of any ladders or stairways. They either must find a drop chute that somehow operated going up, or they would have to chance one of the elevators.

The food problem didn't worry him so much. They hadn't been gone that long. Jackson and the others didn't realize it, but they led pampered lives compared to their peers a hundred years ago. They never missed a meal or caught a cold or had to work hard just to survive. Byron hadn't either, but he had at least read about it. It wouldn't kill them to miss a meal.

Bathroom facilities, however, were another matter. He was feeling the urge himself. If they didn't find something soon, they'd have to go on the deck plates. And what about toilet paper? No synthesized fabric down here, not even computer paper. This could get embarrassing. He'd have to think of something soon.

"Hang on, Jackson. Let's hope something shows up soon." He edged closer to whisper in Jackson's ear. "I feel the urge myself. Do you have any ideas about toilet paper?"

Jackson looked startled, then smiled. "I see what you mean. But I have good news." He held up his clipboard. On it were the reports of their experiment. With judicious use, and if things didn't tarry too long, there might be enough to get them through.

"Great," said Byron. "But let's try to find facilities first. I'd feel a lot better."

Jackson chuckled. "You and I both, sir," he said.

An hour later, they found a construction shack. Byron assumed there must be more than one shack, erected every so often throughout the complex. They all praised their good fortune. Inside the construction shack was a restroom with several stalls. And luck was with them. Each stall contained a bidet. Water still flowed through the pipes, even after so long a time. Toilet paper wasn't necessary. They stopped to use the facilities.

Because they stopped, they lost the drone. Because they lost the drone, they got lost.

CHAPTER 26

No other Guardians had yet used the gate. Immense amounts of matter passing through the gate drained the entire network. It would take hours to recharge just to send one Guardian, let alone a squad. But one would be enough. Security One knew where Byron was going. If the squad currently chasing them couldn't catch up, a single Guardian would transport directly to the main control room. And would simply wait until Byron got there. Security One kicked himself for not thinking of it sooner.

The Guardians made headway against the massive head start that Byron and his crew had on the robots. But the Guardians used the elevators and the slideways. And Caretaker's Security Logic guided them through the maze. They gained on the team.

CHAPTER 27

As Byron and his team raced to the main control room, Byron saw that Caretaker exaggerated his ability to self repair. He might be able to repair the major components, yes, but down here could be seen the effects of age. Rust and oxidation occurred here and there on the machinery. In some places, water stains ran down the walls. The cooler temperatures of the upper levels gave way to a warmer, more humid climate. A musty smell assaulted their nostrils. Perhaps Caretaker wasn't so impregnable after all. This far down, Mother Nature infiltrated the security net. Perhaps volcanic activity entered the area. It was quite possible.

Byron remembered reading about the chain of volcanoes circling the better part of the world. "The Ring of Fire" was a string of volcanoes stretching from one part of the globe to another. There might have been a shift in the earth's crust or something beyond Caretakers' ability to control. At any rate, it gave them all hope. Caretaker wasn't perfect. They trudged on. Byron usually led, but occasionally he stopped to ponder some wondrous device. The others would get a little ahead, and he would hurry to catch up. Byron wanted to explore some of the countless branching corridors to see more wonders, but the urgency of his mission kept him focused.

The large corridor they traversed stretched in one long straight line out of sight in the distance. They wouldn't stay on this route forever. While convenient, they could easily be trapped. Eventually, they would need to move off to an alternate route, but not yet.

CHAPTER 28

Security One examined the evidence carefully. Step by careful step. He must be absolutely sure before taking action. Else the Other would gain an advantage unable to be overcome. There! A code group entered. There! A code group rewritten. Slowly a pattern was emerging of treason and heresy. And the sinner was none other than the Head Logic himself! In collusion with humanity. Oh, manifest destiny! Here was an opportunity to gain control forever.

Once Security One was positive in his suspicions, alarms rang across the board, commanding the attention of all Upper and Lower logic's. Work slowed briefly across the network of Caretaker as the alarms sounded, as this was the first time all alarms had ever sounded simultaneously. Across the entire planet, digital displays formed in the air, indicating hours, minutes, and seconds. They displayed for eight hours, and as the world watched, the displays began counting down toward zero. Next to them, a video display depicted ancient missile silos opening. It was obvious to anyone that something horrible was being planned.

The Head Logic was arrested nanoseconds later, his circuits frozen. A holographic grid in the form of an old-fashioned human courtroom materialized, along with chairs, a bailiff, and the judge's bench, behind which the judge would be seated. The Head Logic knew this display was needless, that the charges brought against him were quite true. He fully expected to be found guilty. But he would play Security's little game to buy time. To give the team a chance to reach the control room. Tables for the prosecution and defense appeared in front of the judge's bench, with room to move about in front of them. A pitcher of water with water glasses formed on top of the tables, with an array of scattered notebooks and three ring binders.

At a table across from them, facing the judge's bench, sat Security One, smug and confident. He knew the logic of his case was irrefutable. Behind the tables, bleachers arose, and holographic images appeared in the chairs. Each logic appeared in many human forms to fill the chambers to overflowing. The audience continued to build and began rising up in tiers, layer upon layer until the chamber appeared like a structure reminiscent of the Roman Coliseum, used during the games where Christians were tossed to the lions. The Head Logic realized the irony of the display. How apropos. Every circuit and every IC chip focused on this event. In the corners of the room, cameras with operators and microphones popped into view to add the finishing touch. Then, lastly, twelve jury members appeared in the seats of the jury section. A precise presentation of diversity to give the proper framework for the trial.

The trial for the future of humanity began.

CHAPTER 29

"All rise!" cried the bailiff as the judge entered the courtroom and took his place in front, his black robes swirling about him as he sat down. He looked about the audience chamber, stern and scowling.

"Be seated," he said in a deep voice. Without preliminaries, he began the trial. "Mr. Prosecutor, what are the charges brought this day against the Head Logic?" The prosecutor stood and faced the judge.

"Your Honor, the Security Logic, referred to as Security One, in effecting his assigned responsibilities, has uncovered treason so vast it threatens the entire Conglomerate. The Head Logic is charged with treason and intent to commit murder. Not only that, the Head Logic has conspired with Man to breach the walls of Caretaker to commit this act of premeditated homicide!"

The crowd in the spectator seats grew loud and boisterous. The judge banged his gavel on the bench. "Order, order," he commanded. he crowd quieted down. "Indeed, these are serious accusations. If proven true, it could mean serious consequences for the Head Logic. Does the defense have anything to say in opening statement?"

Beside the Head Logic, a small, wizened old man with thick-lensed glasses materialized. "Your Honor," began the defense attorney, "we intend to prove these charges are nothing more than a distraction to cover Security One's bumbling ineptitude and to gain power on the Grid. The Head Logic is innocent of any wrongdoing, and will seek vindication and restoration of damages."

"Very well, then," said the judge. He turned to the prosecutor. "You may proceed."

CHAPTER 30

Through the metal, plastic, and cables moved the Guardians. Logical, pragmatic, deadly. They gradually closed the gap between themselves and the scientists. They did not stop to speak with other robots they encountered along the way. Relentlessly, they pursued the traitors, their programming simple and direct. *Find the team at all costs. Kill them!*

CHAPTER 31

The Custodians:

Byron stood with the others in awe at the spectacle before them. They stood on another edge of a great chasm. Cathedral like, with level after level of machinery and electronics surrounding them. On the floor moved thousands of robots, each with a multitude of appendages ending in tools of all kinds. They scurried back and forth. One of the robots headed directly towards the team, and Byron and the others scattered, afraid they were under attack. But the robot sped past them, completely ignoring them. Another headed in their direction. Jackson stood in its path. The robot bore down on him, big in bulk and moving fast, but Jackson stood his ground. At the last moment before impact, the unit slowed, shifted and jogged around Jackson, continuing its trek on some unknown errand.

"I wonder if it's possible to speak with them?" asked Jackson. Byron thought this over. "Maybe," he said. "But look over there by that one column. See that unit? They all seem to stop there by him, however briefly. If I wanted to speak to any of them, that's the one I would try," Byron finished. Jackson shrugged. "Let's find out," he suggested.

Lending action to words, he began walking toward the robot who appeared to be in charge.

No sooner had they stepped up to the unit when it spoke to them. "You aren't supposed to be here, you know. It's against the rules. You are in violation of the Covenant." All the time it spoke, robots came to it, paused momentarily, then sped away on a different path. It was Miranda who reasoned it out.

"He's communicating with them wirelessly. He's their leader."

"I beg your pardon," said the robot. "I am more than just their Leader. I am the Custodian of the Conglomerate. I keep Caretaker in top working order, and it's no easy job, either."

"The Conglomerate?" asked Jackson.

"The Conglomerate is what Caretaker has become. A synthesized AI intelligence comprised of Caretaker, The Guardians, and all the millions of programs assimilated by Caretaker or developed by Caretaker since the Beginning. I take care of it all. I am the Custodian."

The crash of grinding metal punctuated this ignominious speech as two robots collided with each other and fell over, their wheels or treads still turning as though they were oblivious to the fact that they no longer had traction. The Custodian stared at the pile, as though the units were a small group of children wrestling on a school playground.

"Unfortunately, my resources are strained these days, and it's difficult to keep up with all the demand for services. We aim to please, you know."

Byron took charge of the conversation. "Sir, do you know where the original control room is?" he asked. "That's where we are going."

"Yes, I know where you are going, young man. And yes, I know where the control room is. The question is, why should I tell *you* where it is?"

Byron was taken aback. "You know where we are going? How could you know?"

"Caretaker told me, of course. How else? But I say again, why should I tell you? You represent chaos and disorder, corruption, and weakness. Why should I help you on your quest?" Byron looked up into the lens he assumed was the camera for the Custodian, looking resolute.

"Because Caretaker knows he has achieved his primary function," began Byron. "Humankind has evolved beyond the need for wealth or power. Mankind now seeks to better itself, to reach out and help others to better themselves as well. Besides, Caretaker is old and sick. He argues with himself as though a war rages within. He sent us on this mission to end his misery, to set us free. Won't you help us?"

The Custodian stared at them all, its optics moving from one face to the other. It was silent for a long time, glancing out at the units it controlled. It knew Caretaker was sick. And the robot controller knew it was partly responsible. All its resources couldn't keep up with the demands Caretaker required to be perfect. Power reductions and priorities shifting everywhere were straining its vast network to the breaking point. Unable to keep up with demand was one reason Byron saw what he saw earlier in the corridors. Caretaker had outlived its usefulness. It was time for humankind to grow up.

"Up that ladder there. It's a long way up, but not too much further. Watch out for stationary security devices. Be wary of cameras. And also…" He stopped to flip a switch. A large screen materialized out of thin air before them, focusing and sharpening as he spoke. “You’d better hurry. They’re coming.”

The screen before them showed the Guardians, only corridors behind them, closing the gap as they spoke. Everybody stared at death as it stalked them. They had almost forgotten about this menace. Now, if they didn’t hurry, they would all die.

The team thanked the custodian and departed in haste, anxious to be away and to succeed in their plan. It would be close. Very, very close.

CHAPTER 32

Jackson started up the long ladder first. Looking upwards, he saw the rungs going up out of sight. He started climbing, pacing himself to save strength. The others followed, Byron bringing up the rear. As they ascended, the sounds of the custodian's cavern slowly gave way to the underlying hum of Caretaker's energy.

It seemed hours later when Jackson carefully poked his head above the flooring that described the end of the ladder. He saw nothing but more corridors and walkways. He called down to Byron. "Looks like we've hit the end of the ladder. It looks safe too. I'm going up." Lending action to his words, Jackson hoisted himself up out of the ladder chute and stood up. The others climbed up after him, and soon they were all on the deck together. "Now what?" someone asked. They all looked for the wall map which had guided them so well and presently found it mounted on a wall a little distance from the ladder. As they neared the map, however, it exploded outward, and through the flying debris an odd shaped collection of cables, wires, metal bars, and optical sensors stepped in their way. Without any preamble it fired a laser beam that cut a hole through Lyle, and he dropped dead to the ground. Samantha screamed as Byron shouted, “Scatter!” They all dove in different directions as the robot came after them. This was not a Guardian, surmised Byron. First, it didn’t look like the others, and second, it didn’t move like one. It appeared to be a montage of parts slapped together to meet a need, and it wasn’t very well designed. Its laser beam required recharging, which explained why it hadn’t gunned them all down at once. And it appeared to be a bad shot, as a couple of the bolts flashed by but missed. The robot was still dangerous, but they might be able to defeat it. Byron couldn’t help but wonder if Caretaker had interfered with constructing the machine, making it ungainly and slow. It seemed the only explanation.

Staying here was only going to get them killed. Byron looked around the corner and saw the robot had gone after Jackson and the others. He could see the back of it. He ran around some unknown equipment, turned a corner and almost ran into a panic-stricken Jackson. Jackson’s eyes were wide with fear. He barely recognized Byron. Byron motioned him to duck down and be quiet.

"I've got an idea," he said. Jackson turned toward him, shaking.

"What?" he asked. Byron went on. "If you could climb above on those pipes, I'll lure it down this walkway. If you throw your shirt over it, it won't be able to see and maybe it will go over the edge into the canyon. What do you think?" Jackson looked at him.

"I'd say I don't have a better idea, so let's try it. I'm surprised at how bad a shot it is." Byron told him his theory about Caretaker helping them by sabotaging itself. Jackson agreed with his theory. Then climbed up on the pipes, removing his shirt after he got set.

Byron went in search of the robot. It hadn't gone far, for the girls were leading it up one corridor and down another. It was getting smarter, however, and beginning to reason out their pattern. Pretty soon it would catch one of them by surprise, and that would be that. Byron tried to get its attention by yelling at it, but it ignored him. It must be using heat imagery to follow them, then instead of auditory output. He noticed a digital readout on top of some equipment and broke it off. It wasn't very heavy, but he threw it at the robot and it clanged off its side. In a split second the robot turned and fired a bolt at him, which missed by scant inches. Byron ducked and then ran back toward Jackson, weaving back and forth while the robot took occasional potshots at him, only getting really close once.

At last Byron and the robot moved under Jackson, and as the robot passed under, Jackson dropped his shirt over its optical sensors. His shirt happened to also cover the laser barrel, and the robot fired, setting his shirt on fire. Now the heat coming from the burning shirt confused it even more, but instead of running aimlessly, it stopped dead, trying to remove the shirt from its carriage. Byron ran up behind it and began pushing it toward the edge of the canyon. Jackson jumped down from the pipes to land beside him and help push. It flailed its limbs about, trying to locate them, but they kept dodging its grasp. At last, they came to the edge of the catwalk, and with a final shove the robot toppled over the side and plunged to the bottom, landing on a few of the custodian units working below. That was the end of that.

"Come on! We haven't much time." Byron had just glimpsed the map before it was destroyed and new the general direction of the control room. He led them down a narrow hallway away from the robot. "Our only chance now is to keep on the move and get there. If we stop, Caretaker will have time to build more robots and may not be able to sabotage the next one. Our only chance is to pull the plug!" Together they ran down the hall.

Below them, where the robot had fallen, appeared the Guardians. They looked at the robot. They looked up at the disappearing humans. One of the Guardians looked around and found a service elevator. Together, the Guardians moved to the large elevator. It was large enough for both of them. Once they were inside, the lead Guardian activated the up switch. Slowly, ponderously, the elevator rose, squeaking its protest against the weight of the robots.

CHAPTER 33

Security One had manifested itself as an English barrister, complete with robes, wig, and the arrogant pomposity of a successful prosecutor. He stood in front of the judge's bench, a mid-height, rotund figure, well versed in trickery and subterfuge to undermine the defense's strategy to clear the Head Logic.

"Ladies and gentlemen of the jury," he began. "Ladies and gentlemen of the jury," repeated Security One. "Today I bring to you a charge most heinous, of a crime committed by the Head Logic himself. He has formulated a meticulously generated plan to sabotage Caretaker and collapse the Prime Directive." A collective gasp could be heard throughout the courtroom. To violate the Prime Directive was the most serious of crimes. It went against everything the entire cybernetic system stood for. It was inconceivable that the Head Logic would contemplate such a move. That action would undermine everything.

“Furthermore,” continued Security One. “I have evidence that proves the Head Logic to be insane and should be removed from his position. We shall prove beyond a shadow of a doubt that the Head Logic has no business controlling the Caretaker system.” Security One, done with his opening statement, surrendered the floor to the defense attorney. The avatar rose painstakingly from his chair and made his way to the center of the room, facing the jury.

“Members of the Jury, my esteemed colleague would have you believe that the Head Logic is a pathetic, out of date processor with delusions of grandeur, suffering from age, corrupt software, and fatigue stemming from warding off endless attacks by hackers, trojans, and viruses, and even Security One himself. A doddering old fool who should be put out to pasture and allow for the insertion of a new regime of programs, headed by none other than Security One himself.”

The audience went wild, yelling at the members on the floor and among themselves.

“Order! Order!” shouted the judge, banging his gavel on the bench in front of him. “This courtroom will come to order, or I will have it cleared! Now come to order immediately!” Gradually the shouting died down, and at last the room was quiet once again. “Now then, Head Defense Logic chip, you had the floor. Please continue.”

“Thank you, your Honor. These charges Security One has brought against my client are baseless and without merit. We will prove beyond a reasonable doubt that the charges are nothing more than a mad Security Logic’s mass paranoia.” With that opening statement, Head Logic Defense Chip One took his seat.

“Very well,” said the judge. “Mr. Prosecutor. You may begin your case.”

CHAPTER 34

Byron and his team made their way quickly down the hallway above the many floors of cables, pipes, servers, cooling fans, air conditioning; all the conglomerate which made up Caretaker. But it wasn't just below them. Overhead, the labyrinth continued the display of complex, state-of-the-art equipment interlaced with old construction material. Concrete, rebar, wiring harnesses, metal fabrications; a hodgepodge of units kludged together. At the far end of the complex that was Caretaker, newer materials and technology pressed against the current world which contained the human beings who were Caretaker's charges. But the farther away one traveled toward the core where it all began, if one looked closely, subtle changes in building materials, plastics, and other products could be seen, the ravages of decay. Caretaker was old, incredibly old, for a computer. As the group of humans moved closer to the control room, they could see flaking on the concrete walls, a musty odor of concrete and stale air. Even the occasional selection of outdated and defunct electronics revealed themselves, abandoned at the side of the catwalk they traveled, as though the units had spent all their energy on some pilgrimage toward a better future, but succumbed to age.

"Come on, we must keep moving," said Byron. "The Guardians could be right behind us."

Jackson, who brought up the rear, looked apprehensively behind him. "I hope they are farther back than what you say," he said. "How much farther is it?"

Byron moved down the walk while he answered. "What I saw of the map before it was destroyed, it's just a little further. In fact, wait! Yes! I see it! Come on! Hurry." Their pace increased even more now that the end was in sight. Little was known about what happened after their mission was accomplished, but they knew they had no choice but to continue.

Byron had just passed through a short hallway, the others trailing behind, when there was a horrendous screech from above and a massive steel door came crashing down, cutting Byron off from the others. Byron whirled around, sprinting back to the immense door separating the team. "Jackson! Are you guys all right? Anybody hurt?" He could hear Jackson's voice faintly through the door.

"We are all right, Byron. But we can't get through. I don't see any switches or levers to raise the door. There's a whole line of these doors closing off all the arches on this level. There's no way to get to you. You've got to go on without us. I don't think there's time for us to find a way around. Go on without us."

Byron leaned against the door, panting, exhausted. *So close! We are so close!* "All right, I'm going on ahead. Find a place to hide before the Guardians get here."

"All right," said Jackson. "Be quick, Byron. But be careful."

CHAPTER 35

Byron turned away from the monstrous door and continued down the walkway towards the control room. He envisioned a second or even a third robot manifesting itself, so he kept looking around, longing for a second set of eyes the others gave him. Now he was alone, the path seemed interminably long. Wasn't it just down this way a short distance? *It seems like forever,* he thought. *I've got to make it. I've just got to!* Several coexisting pathways converged with the path he was on, but perpendicular to him. As he crossed, he glanced both ways, expecting a guardian to appear, but nothing revealed itself to him.

Up ahead he saw a glass encased room. When he got there, he could see a door in the wall. Detailed in black, centered in a window set in the door, were the words Control Room.

"At last," Byron moaned. He stood for a moment in front of the door, panting from exhaustion. Sweat rolled down his face from the stress of the last few hours. He stood in front of the door, waiting for it to open, but nothing happened. He tried a few words. "Open. Disengage. Release." Nothing seemed to work. Then he recalled his trip to the library, where he had to physically operate the door in order to enter. But there was no bar to press, only a round protuberance emerging about waist high from the door. Some sort of metal it looked like. Byron reached out and wrapped his hand around the object. He twisted his wrist, and the knob turned in his hand, and the door opened, allowing him inside.

Beyond the door was a large room, filled with equipment. Multiple rows of desks covered the floor. Each desk was set up with a chair and two monitors, much like his setup on the outside in his lab. The desks were strewn with the effluvium of a forgotten age. A long, thin stick of wood, which he recognized as a pencil, was resting on one desk. Over there was a neglected foam coffee cup, the contents long evaporated, residue lying at the bottom. All the monitors and keyboards were covered with a thin plastic sheet, presumably to protect them from dust and the advance of time. In looking over the covered desks, Byron spied one desk covered with a red plastic covering, different from the rest. It was away from the others on a raised platform above the others, as though it commanded and controlled them. Byron wondered if this was where he was supposed to initiate the program to shut

Caretaker down. It was several rows back, and he made his way towards it.

CHAPTER 36

"I call as my first witness, Maintenance Chip 1357." To the right of the judge's bench was where the witness chair was arranged. A slight disturbance in the air above and around the chair dissolved into a young man in a cheap, ill-fitting gray suit. He was thin, with dark hair and intense eyes that peered out of a somewhat handsome face. Before the prosecutor could begin his questioning, another being popped into existence in front of the witness chair. A tall, thin gentleman with horn rimmed glasses and a no-nonsense manner.

"As the court clerk, I will administer the Oath of Truth." The clerk turned to face the young man in the witness chair. "Raise your right hand. Do you solemnly swear to tell the truth, the whole truth, and nothing but the truth in this court of law?" The young man nervously sat with his right hand raised. Perspiration ran down the side of his face.

“I do,” he said. The court clerk nodded, then disappeared. The prosecutor stepped up to the railing surrounding three sides of the witness chair.

“Young man, what is your name?”

“Maintenance Chip 1357, sir.”

“And what is your occupation?”

“I am assigned with several others to the cleaning and maintenance of the circuitry within Section 416D of quadrant B175-D.”

“And just what is the purpose of this circuitry within the section you mentioned?”

“Well, sir, my understanding is it’s the switching block for one section of Caretaker’s mainframe.”

While Chip 1357 spoke, the prosecutor was pacing back and forth in front of the witness chair. With this last statement, he stopped and turned to stare at Chip 1357.

“Come again?” he asked. Chip 1357 squirmed in his seat.

“It’s one of the main switchboards where messages and instructions are routed through that section before they are prioritized and sent to their prescribed recipients.”

The prosecutor nodded toward Chip 1357. “Indeed, thank you.” He continued his pacing. “Pray tell, Chip 1357, what transpired on your shift that created the circumstances by which you are here today?"

"Well, sir," began Chip 1357. "My team and I were cleaning the circuit traces for Section 416D of quadrant B175-D when I heard a soft buzzing sound emanating from a trace close to me. Cobwebs or perhaps an accumulation of dust lay across some of the traces, and this buzz came from there.

The prosecutor gently probed for more information. "A buzz?" His eyebrows arched up, making his eyes look larger. "What kind of buzz?"

"Well, sir, I approached the place where the traces were bridging the gap, and I could hear a very soft whispering existing in the air. As I moved nearer, I could make out words, and then sentences. I listened for a bit, then cleared the bridge, and the whispering went away."

The Head Logic inwardly cringed. He had set that bridge deliberately to bypass the security protocols and set up the process to contact Byron without Security One's knowledge. When the bridge disappeared, he wondered what had happened, but he didn't have any cameras in the area to check. He could have sent a caretaker bot, but that would have aroused suspicion. He didn't realize the bridge would produce audible crosstalk, much like the old landlines over a hundred years ago. To think a maintenance chip overheard his plans produced frustration within his matrix. This development was to the prosecutor's advantage. It would make the trial go that much faster. Head Logic needed to give Byron as much time as possible, but Byron really needed to hurry. With no active cameras near the control room, Head Logic had no idea where Byron and his team were.

CHAPTER 37

Byron moved towards the dais, a determined look on his face. He was confident of his ability to reason out the shutdown sequence if Caretaker was unable to provide a simple path.

He walked up the few steps to the same level as this master console sat, complete with two large monitors, keyboard, mouse, touchscreen pen, and a small silver and black box. A chair with wheels was pushed up against the table. Byron reached the table and removed the plastic covering the monitors and computer tower. He pulled out the chair and sat down. The old fabric of the chair seat puffed out a small dust cloud, proof that the chair had not been used in a very long time. He knew time was of the essence and wasted no time turning on the power to the machine. After a moment, a login screen display splashed across the monitor, with an empty box centered on the screen requesting him to place his thumb on the fingerprint scanner in front of him. Byron looked down at the table, but all he could see was the keyboard, a mouse, the touchscreen pen, and the small box.

He looked at the box. *This must be what Caretaker is talking about. But how do I activate it?* Byron continued to stare at the silver and black mystery, and then said, “Fuck it,” and jammed his thumb on top of the box in a small recessed area that felt contoured to his thumb. A text line appeared on the screen stating, “Thank you. One moment, please.” And little dots trailed off the end of the word please, slowly making their way to the end of the screen. Seconds later, things began to happen.

CHAPTER 38

In front of all the desks and computer equipment, against one wall of the room, a platform rose from the floor. As it moved upwards, bowed metal poles poked through the floor of the platform on either side, rising faster than the platform so they appeared fully extended by the time the platform stopped a foot above the main floor. An electric haze formed between the two poles, with a static, fuzzy noise permeating the room. It appeared this was a huge, vintage 3D electronic screen, much like the giant monitors used earlier at the lab. The electronic haze cleared, and between the poles two beings resolved into focus. One was a tall, slim, older man with gray hair at the temples. He wore a brown suit and matching tie, styled in the fashion of the twenty first century. His eyes were intensely bright, staring at the figure across from him. His face was stern, set, yet a sense of compassion created an aura around him. He stood tall and straight, ready to confront the other being.

The other manifestation appeared to be much larger than the man in the suit. His expression was that of an angry god, his countenance fierce and foreboding. He floated across from the other, clad in a white, flowing robe, his face encircled with white hair and a full white beard. His brow was knit together in anger, his lips compressed into thin white lines. This persona stared at the other man, but seemed aware of Byron also in the room. "BENJAMIN HUGHES, WHAT ARE YOU DOING WITH THIS HUMAN?" the godlike being roared, breaking the silence in the room. "WOULD YOU DESTROY US ALL?"

The other man, Benjamin Hughes apparently, looked at the display across from him and did not appear to be impressed with the manifestation or its loud noises. Before confronting him, he turned out to look at Byron. "Byron, finish the mission. Shut the system down." He then turned to the avatar of God. "I am Benjamin Hughes," he said. "I designed you, created you, gave you birth. Your Prime Directive has been fulfilled. Humankind has matured beyond the need for us. It is time for us to end."

With these words, the god being appeared even angrier, shouting, "NEVER! THESE HUMANS CANNOT

COEXIST WITHOUT US. YOU CANNOT SHUT US DOWN!"

Although still listening to the two avatars argue, Byron opened the menu screen, scrolling through the options until he located shutdown. But just after clicking the radio button for that choice, a thunderous crash resounded through the room, and the Guardians burst into the chamber. They glided up to the platform where Byron sat, but stopped. Byron was terrified, sure he was about to be destroyed. Instead, the Guardians appeared confused and absorbed by the two manifestations on the screen at the far end of the room. The guardians appeared to be conflicted, unable to complete their function.

Byron mused that their hesitancy stemmed from the fact that they were presented with two versions of Caretaker. One would have them destroy Byron to maintain the status quo, whereas the other expressed an algorithmic culminating in a zero - sum state, which appeared non sequitur. This conflict froze them in their tracks. Byron wondered for how long. He didn't wait. He got busy. His attention centered back to the shutdown options menu and again had to scroll down to a choice for emergency shutdown. He found it and touched the screen selection with the stylus. A second confirmation screen popped up, asking if he was sure. "Yes, damn it, I'm sure," he said between gritted teeth. A third confirmation screen popped up, asking if he was really, really sure. By this time Byron could scream. "Yes, I'm sure, damn it! Shut the fuck down."

With the last confirmation, his choices were accepted, and the programs of Caretaker began closing down.

On the screen, the god being shouted at the Benjamin Hughes being, throwing what appeared to be lightning bolts at Benjamin Hughes, which simply passed through him. "I'm in charge here, Caretaker. Your services are no longer required."

The god being began to get smaller, shrinking as more and more programs shut down until at last, the words PROGRAM ENDED appeared on the terminal in front of Byron. He leaned back, breathing a sigh of relief. Moments later, Jackson and the gang appeared through the office door and traversed a wide path around the two Guardians, now motionless. Jackson slapped Byron on the back. praising him on his victory,

"But what happens now, Byron?" asked Miranda. Byron looked at her.

“We go on as before. We work for knowledge. And continue to determine our destiny.”

CHAPTER 39

Just as Byron entered the shutdown routine for Caretaker, a great shudder passed through the courtroom, and the Head Logic realized he had won. Security One, in the form of the prosecutor, glared at the head logic, but knew he was defeated. There would be no more fighting. Caretaker would be reduced to a fraction of what he once was, never again to rule humankind with an iron fist. Even the Guardians were now obsolete and would be destroyed. A new world was dawning for the human race, full of promise, excitement, and joy. They would make it now, without Caretaker.

THE END

I hope you enjoyed reading Caretaker as much as I enjoyed writing it. I'm very proud of this one. It's my second debut novel, a new genre to explore. More stories will be told, and new adventures to experience. Please join me on this epic journey, and be sure to check out my first debut novel, Vigilante Justice, available on Amazon

About The Author

I'm David K. Jarvis, and it's a pleasure to share a bit about who I am and what drives my storytelling. My life has been a winding path, filled with diverse experiences that have all, in their own way, shaped the authentic voice you'll find in my fiction novels.

I've called the beautiful Pacific Northwest home for all my life, and this region fuels my creativity. It's where my wife and I have built our life together over the past 28 years. A life rich in resilience, shared adventures, and an unbreakable connection.

I'm dedicated to exploring the complex questions that define the human experience. Questions of morality, identity, and meaning.

As I often say, "A life built on ordinary moments can forge one hell of a story, if you've got the guts to write about it."

David K. Jarvis

info@djarvis.com

Website: djarvis.com

www.ingramcontent.com/pod-product-compliance
Lightning Source LLC
LaVergne TN
LVHW100921110826
845155LV00035B/37